The Strategy of Love

(Guardians of Refuge Book 2)

By

Alyssa Bailey

To my personal Military Man. You are always my inspiration because you are my first, last, and only true love.

Description

PHOTOJOURNALIST KAYLA Rhea exposes injustices in the world and takes chances with her life to do it. It has always been an acceptable risk until she is abducted, bringing Army Strategist River Bennett crashing back into her life.

Their passions run hot, and as their relationship heats up, so do the threats on her life from international traffickers she has exposed. River believes he can eradicate the risk with a little help from his military connections, but as more clues are revealed, the danger only grows.

Kayla's life is in mortal jeopardy when they discover the threat is closer than anyone imagined. When it is discovered that the most devastating source of danger could be Kayla herself, River needs to use all his training and experience to find their happily ever after.

Chapter One

The screaming silence made his skin crawl. Major Jonathan River Bennett III tried to control the shiver in response to his sweat as it rolled slowly down his hot, sticky back. River's entire body itched from the heat, plant-life, and insects surrounding him, attaching to him, making stillness a challenge. The urge to scrape something hard and angular across his skin to relieve the torturous surface irritations became agonizing. River couldn't scratch, couldn't move. His life may depend on it.

River wanted to be anywhere but here on his second 'last mission' for the U.S. military in a month. He couldn't believe the timing. Literally, moments before his special operations unit left Mogadishu, the call came through, putting his team back into the playing field.

Through his trained peripheral vision, River looked over at the men he'd brought on this mission. Katz, Grady, Jonas, and Martine were his family, and a better one would be hard to find. Saunders, their pilot, was waiting for the call to return to take them home. They were all going off-line after this stopover. These same men had completed their previous assignment so well, no one knew they'd been in country at all except the team and their Command. The target was on his way home, just as this Delta Force Team should have been.

Somalia was not a place any pampered or unprepared man or woman should find themselves without prior education. The imprudent senator, his equally foolish wife, and the man who kidnapped her would all end today with a different perspective on life. River allowed his subconscious mind to wander as he waited for the perpetrator's next move. He had learned to watch, listen, and plan at the same time. His mother had said multi-tasking was a female trait. He'd practiced it until it was second nature to him.

It was apparent the young senator's wife had no concept of countries and cultures more desperate and violent than those free, democratic ones she had visited thus far. It had found her in predictable trouble. If Mrs. Gregovich thought going with her husband to Somalia's governmental center would be a good learning experience, an adventure to tell all her friends back home, she would be right. She'd ignored good experience talking when the U.S. government, Somalia's government, and her husband had advised against the trip.

His attention was taken when there was a slight, almost imperceivable movement to his right. Martine had seen something of interest and shifted slightly before giving the signal. Stand down. Nothing of interest. River's mind veered back to their target.

Mrs. Gregovich expected the military would ensure her protection no matter how many times and ways she was told not to rely on that. The military presence consisted of trained soldiers, a peace-keeping force for essential personnel, not as bodyguards to foolish people. That small company had military and physical limitations, which became glaringly obvious after the woman arrived in-country. River wondered if they could bill for services rendered.

Before sunset on day two, she had worn her jewelry in public through one of the marketplaces and was promptly kidnapped. Publicly, the U.S. government denounced the act but shrugged their shoulders behind closed doors. They did, however, put in a call to River's superiors privately. Neither the Somalian government nor the U.S. government wanted a political black eye; that's why River's group was called in.

While River believed that if he was given half a chance to put a strategy together, he could be successful in just about anything he put his hand to, there was little planning time for this stopover. It would have to be a plan "A" with a plan "B" backup. Plan "C" was run like hell, officially called falling back to regroup. He'd rarely ever gone there, and only when it was obvious their mission was too compromised to succeed.

They were on their way home, and since it was an in and out exfil involving one person and one overzealous kidnapper, they made an exception to help. For that reason only, and not that their colonel had already committed them to the task, River diverted his men. His team was sitting in yet another God-forsaken hellhole waiting for the moment of movement.

"It's your last time in-country, Bennett, on the government's nickel. Enjoy the adios."

"I've had enough, Colonel, but I'll save your sorry ass one more time, sir."

The longtime friends laughed as they signed off. "Steak and whiskey on me this weekend."

"You know it," said River. He wasn't laughing now. Another quick visual sweep told him they would be waiting a little longer.

God, he'd be glad to get back to his too big for a single man house. It had been a gift from his parents when he joined the military so he would have a place to call home. When River turned twelve, the family of four and his father's entourage had moved to Cache Island, Alaska. At first, it had been for safety. Protecting your family on an out of the way island in Alaska was easier than downtown anywhere. It had turned out to be a good business move and a great place to live.

River brought his head back into the game. Soon he was alerted to the hut they had identified as holding their target. What had started as a single kidnapper had turned into more. Just how many were involved, he wasn't sure. Several men had gone in and out over the last half hour. Inside, a shuffle ensued, then a man left the small building and continued into the barren land, showing no signs of returning. It couldn't be that easy, could it? They had estimated three men were left, but they weren't sure. An unidentified someone had stood in the window continuously until now. In case the exiting man was going for reinforcements, River needed to adjust his thinking.

Giving the signal, each man went their own way, following the plan mapped out for them. River took his station at the only window in the shack. Night was falling. The glass was cracked, grubby, and cumbersome to see through. However, the small amount of light it afforded inside was just enough. The woman looked to be about thirty-five, with what must have been clean and coffered hair before all this happened. She wasn't alone. Two other men were guarding her. One of them headed for the exit.

Quick as the wind, Katz took out the captor as he stepped outside the building. Jonas, River, and Martine stormed the little room and secured the target. They took down the second captor. Grady, once he saw things were under control, took off toward the first abductor.

"Mrs. Gregovich are you hurt?" asked River, keeping his voice low as he untied and shuffled her out of the cramped room, leaving the tied kidnappers behind. He knew the two men wouldn't be waking, but better civilians didn't know his guys had killed them in their presence. One less thing to have nightmares over.

She shook her head, and that worked for him. He took a cursory appraisal and agreed she hadn't been harmed, physically. As they headed out, the woman was quiet at first. Grady met up with them within ten minutes, and the trek back to civilization began. It was only a couple of hours away. River hoped that the woman was able to get there under her own power. She looked fit enough, but he knew you couldn't always tell.

His team was polite and careful but as they went through rough terrain, he thought about finding a more comfortable but less direct route. Unfortunately, Mrs. Gregovich had begun to complain about the accommodations, and the fastest way out was best. Unbelievably, she wasn't the only civilian who was less than thankful for the way they were rescued. Incredible, really, but they had delivered her safely to her husband. They were preparing to set up their transport home when River's phone went off.

"Bennett, I need you to stay in-country and run one more op for me."

"Shit. You're determined to make me work for my exit."

"Nah, you're still on the roster to ETS out in six months. Now here's the skinny on this one. She's the daughter of a good friend of mine."

"Yeah, I figured it was something personal. What the hell is going on that we're allowing our women to come to dangerous places, do stupid things, and then we go to great lengths to save them? Don't suppose we can leave her there?"

"You aren't serious."

River was silent.

"She's the daughter of Command Sergeant Major Rhea, retired. He's a *very* good friend of mine."

More silence.

"Dammit, River."

"No, I'm not serious. You know that. But I am serious about considering paddling this woman's ass for endangering herself. How old is she now?" Damn, just the thought of her long amber-gold hair and spirited behavior made River dream of comforters and room service.

"Now? You know her?"

"I met her when she was in her first year of college."

River remembered what a beauty she was even then. He could only imagine how stunning she was now. His cock twitched.

"She participated in a meet and greet when her father was accepting his new position. She was in high school then and the darling of the room. Too smart and too sassy for her own good. I knew she'd probably turn out to be a hell-raiser, although she was well protected and on a tight leash then, so what happened? How old did you say?"

"Twenty-six, and from what I understand, you'd have to stand in line for the paddling," said his friend with a chuckle. "She's Rob's only daughter. Kayla is the youngest with two older brothers, both previous military, who adore her, as you have already discovered."

"Later, I actually met her at my family's Foundation Gala. We didn't get to spend much time getting to know each other, but she seemed to still have a good head on her shoulders."

"I guess she is just another pampered woman who thought to come to a country where women didn't survive easily and where violence is commonplace made for an excellent vacation spot. I thought she was brighter than this. She certainly seemed to be. You need to get smarter friends with more intelligent family members, *sir*."

"I hear you, but that isn't what's going on here. Kayla is there with a benevolent society and smart as a whip. She is well trained, well equipped, and well-meaning. Rob is in the security business and knows the drill."

"AKA for a mercenary group. Why aren't his guys doing the retrieval?"

"Because you're there and they aren't. Rhea's guys are wheels up in another hour and will be there tomorrow afternoon. They'll definitely have your back if necessary. And, for your FYI, they don't typically do mercenary gigs."

"Not typically. What about now?"

"Rob had it arranged for eyes on the ground, but there was a mix up in the communication of the group's travel arrangements. The women arrived before their security. The group has never been bothered before, but something changed this trip, and Kayla, plus the other three women with her, were abducted. It appeared a setup, all put in motion far in advance of their arrival, by someone in the know. Only the group was told their travel plans had changed, not their detail."

Yep, he imagined the Sergeant was already three-fourths of the way to the answer. If Rhea had raised his daughter like River heard he'd commanded his troops, she wouldn't be this reckless. Hell, this was a shit hole for females of all ages, but a young, blue-eyed American was a prime target. In this world of commodities, she was prime real estate. The sergeant should have used more traditional ways to send his message, if needed, to keep her safe.

River knew if his woman or daughter, if he ever got that lucky, put herself in harm's way on purpose, he would use whatever method necessary to keep her safe. Engaging in hand to butt combat with a lovely woman was not out of the question. If it was sanctioned by the woman, it was one of the things that excited River. It had never intimidated him to administer a little discipline to clear the air or stir the juices.

He remembered the last time he'd seen Kayla. He was just taking a break after a tough strategic session on a mission that brought everyone home, barely. The Foundation was having their annual Christmas Benefit, and he wasn't up for smiling at everyone. He wouldn't have been there if his mother hadn't insisted there would be some fun ladies in attendance.

"It would mean so much to your father and me."

When he saw Kayla, he had to have her. She was young. Still in college from what he overheard. Perfect. Old enough to have a play session with and young enough not to want a commitment. He didn't do those because no woman deserved to live with a man that was either gone or had his head consumed with the next mission.

"River, have you met Kayla Rhea? Kayla, this is my son, River." Mrs. Bennett smiled at Kayla and said in a stage whisper, "He's a good dancer." He watched his mother walk away.

With a great show of formal dignity, delivered with a flourish, he asked, "Well, Miss Kayla Rhea, would you like to dance?" He ruined the effect with a slight smile.

"Yes, thank you." She replied with equal formality and a twinkle in her eye. As he took her arm, she smiled.

He'd received a call as the dance was ending. *On-standby*. That happened a lot. It was likely they would be released soon. That was good. He could get some alone time with her before anything hit his leisure time.

"Would you like to go somewhere to talk? I'd like to know more about you."

She shocked him. "Sure, my way. Do you have somewhere we could, um, relax out of sight?"

His cock jumped, and his mind shifted into stealth mode. Kayla was a sassy young thing, but he could tame sass. He was used to getting his way, but he could play the game. River exited the hotel ballroom discretely. *Too young* flashed across his brain. At the elevators, his hand at the small of her back, he asked, "Tell me your age again?"

"Twenty-one. Legal in all states."

"I'm only worried about this one, sweetheart. Have you done this before?" Suddenly his protective side sprang up.

She turned amused eyes to meet his. "Had sex?" her laugh bubbled over. "Oh, yes. Not very good sex, mind you, but you're going to change that, aren't you?"

"I hope so. No, my question was, have you picked men up before?"

For the first time, her stance stiffened, and she gave him a doubtful look. "Is that what I did? I thought it was mutual. If it isn't..."

He leaned down and took those lips that he needed to taste. Mmm, like honey, sweet and smooth. "Oh, it's mutual, sweetheart, but I should paddle your butt for being so naughty at your age. What would your father say?"

"He isn't here. And like I said, adult." River almost regretted his one and done rule. He kissed her again until the elevator opened. Maybe... His phone rang.

"Hello." With a heavy sigh, River turned to Kayla. "I apologize, I need to go. Duty calls and all that. I truly would like to see you again."

She had smiled and said all the appropriate words, but he knew she didn't believe him, and he didn't have the luxury of time to correct her thinking. He returned her to the ballroom, took his leave from his mother, letting her know she should check to make sure Kayla really understood. Then he was gone. That had been the one and only experience with Miss Kayla Rhea.

Now she was in trouble. River finished his call after acquiring all the intel available and verifying his orders. They showered and indulged in a large, hot meal before he broke the news to his teammates.

Martine, the team member closest to the Major's own age, said, "I've met Sergeant Major Rhea before. He's good people. His men and women respected him. He was good to work with even though I wasn't under his Command. He's got to be pissed. Hell, yeah, I'll get his daughter." Not that it was a request, but it was better if they all agreed.

Jonas, always looking for a bed warmer, asked, "Is she cute?"

"I guess we'll find out," said River. "However, it won't matter to you because there is no hooking up with the rescued." He made a mental note Jonas was not going to be the one to take care of Miss Rhea. He didn't want to think of anyone but himself with Kayla's long hair wrapped around his hand as he anchored her in place for his exploring. First, he'd swat that sassy ass and wouldn't that get them both hot. Her mews of pseudo distress pulling him closer to her lips. He'd...

"Hey, Bennett, you good?" asked Jonas.

River nodded. "Okay, listen up. These are the details." River concentrated on getting them prepared to do a snatch and run.

The guys went about acquiring new supplies, sleeping as they could, while River checked his gear, cleaned his guns, and took a power nap. They were all sweating by the time they were repacking their go-bags. The meager efforts of the air conditioner were adequate, but not when you were moving around. The team cleaned their weapons while listening to River put together their new strategy for this mission. After they had agreed on the tactic to recover the group, he assigned each their task, but the guys knew what they were doing before he verbalized it. It was merely a formality. Each soldier had their strengths, and River rarely went outside of those. They worked well together after spending the last year as one working unit.

The sun had not yet set, giving the team another chance to catch as many minutes of sleep as they could as they waited for nightfall. River tried but only caught snatches of sleep. He couldn't settle his mind. Something told him to be extra careful. Maybe he was just tired.

As he stared at the bug crawling up the wall, he thought of home. Before this mission, he had vied for and gotten a coveted assignment to the local multi-service unit on Port Refuge.

It was on Quartz Island, the one next to Cache Island that housed his home. It was where he lived as much of the year as he could manage. Quartz Island belonged to the Federal Government, where the joint agencies had a great training center for civilians and the military.

Command was clear when they gave him the assignment. "We hope you'll stick around and work for us. If not in your present position, as a civilian with your experience."

The site also supported the Alaskan southern coast for all kinds of search and rescue. He could volunteer or decide to take them up on their offer to work for them in the civilian world.

River had spent the last decade more out of the country than in, but he enjoyed adding more bells and whistles to his property when he was home. It was time to find out what life would be like without the lives of whole companies on his shoulders. He wondered how long it would take him to return to a regular sleep pattern rather than living on snatches of sleep amongst bugs, heat, and hoping to hear English.

He tried to always spend his downtime in his home, if possible. It was a short, two-hour flight from Seattle to Port Refuge, Alaska, and he took advantage of it. The foundation was run out of their Seattle office because it needed to be, but the operations' brain lived on Cache Island.

After most missions, he was ready to go again when he had a few weeks down, but River didn't feel the least inclined to leave the country anytime soon. This coming home would signal his final landing on U.S. soil under government orders. Time to turn the page, that is, if he could quit getting these damn last-minute call-outs. His mind was back on the golden beauty again. What was she thinking, getting on a plane without her protection?

Time to change life direction and start looking to see what his home town had in the way of eligible women. River hadn't been looking for more than a one-night stand for so long, he no longer knew if he could do two dates in a row with the same woman. Hell, he didn't even know what his type was anymore, but if he had one, Kayla Rhea was definitely it. Or his image of her was.

His mind circled back to the mission. It was game on. What little sleep River got would have to carry him until they found the women in whatever state they were in. He hoped they weren't too late. He needed there to be a happy ending for his third "last mission." He also prayed his unease over this rescue was just tiredness and anticipation of going home, not a premonition.

Chapter Two

Kayla Rhea hit the ground again, her hands and knees already cut, torn and bleeding from the rough treatment and the insanely fast pace her captors insisted on maintaining. She looked over at her three companions and winced. Maeve looked worse than Kayla felt. At twenty-nine, Sandraya was a happy go lucky blonde who would do whatever she could to make the world a brighter place. She had lost her shine as soon as the first abductor squeezed her breast hard.

That was the first contrived time that Kayla fell. She launched herself into the assaultive man. She was soundly smacked, but her brothers had taught her well. She changed her stance, and it was more of a glancing blow. It hurt but was nothing compared to her brothers' roughhousing with her. She played the part to keep the men thinking she was a weak American girl. She knew she needed to wait for the right moment, and their captors' expectations played a huge role.

The second time was because of a tree root; the third time she fell was for a similar reason as Sandraya's, only this time it was to help Rosa, the youngest girl in their party. Rosa could speak several languages, but her Arabic wasn't as good as Kayla's. Again, thanks to her brothers and father. The military had given the men in her family skills they readily passed on to her, sometimes insistently. Today she was thankful. Kayla was competent enough in Arabic to catch most of the conversations between their captors. The hard part was not letting the men know by showing any reactions.

The women continued to struggle to keep up with their captors, but the one most in danger had to be Maeve. She was in her forties and had a strawberry mark that extended from her right temple to her cheekbone. Her warm brown complexion did a fair job of hiding it, but the men made no secret that it disgusted them. It was a defect in their eyes, causing them to treat her accordingly when they found themselves near her.

Kayla did what she could to put herself between Maeve and the men. Sometimes she had no choice but to pick which side of the group she walked, protecting the one in the most danger of harm. She studied the men and decided who was the most dangerous, likely it was Madan for touching. She stationed herself between Maeve and the crazy one. It helped but didn't alleviate all the abuse. When Rosa's shirt was ripped by Magan, Kayla turned to see what she could do and felt fire scorch over her scalp.

Ahmed, the most erratic kidnapper because of his fury, the one she had stationed herself near for over an hour, had yanked her hair so hard, she was surprised she had any still attached. The yelp of pain and rush of tears that rose from behind her nose leaked from her eyes. Kayla couldn't fake or hide that response. It served two purposes: one, to stop the assault on Rosa because the sound Kayla had released gave away their position. Two, the men stopped moving to hide and presumably regroup, thereby giving the women a few moments of rest.

Maeve, who had held up until Kayla yelped, was trembling, as were the other women. For the first time since a man had picked them up, acting as though he were the assigned driver, Kayla realized she might not survive this encounter. Kayla's camera had been wrenched from her as she exited the taxi on the edge of a scary section of town. This was a setup. It had to be. Too many things had gone wrong or eerily fit in place for this to all be a coincidence. The second thing she thought of was, Sarge would be pissed. Not just ticked off, seriously demonic. And she wished with all her heart he was with her right now.

This was her fourth year in this part of the world, the second year her father knew about the trips. It took her two years to gather her nerve to tell him. That and her photos outed her when they made international markets. They were used in an exposé about the violence against the youth in this part of Africa. The village girls were violated in every way one could desecrate a woman until most died from the horrors. Boys were conscripted into the militant groups.

This time, her father practically frothed at the mouth, forbidding her to go and only partially relenting when she gave him the control he needed. Not because Command Sergeant Major Rhea, United States Army, Retired, didn't trust her skill set, but that he knew the world she was traveling to wouldn't respect or care about it. Somalia and the surrounding countries were a hotbed of violence and corruption. Her brother Taren called it the snake pit of hell. To tell the truth, she was relieved to have her dad orchestrating part of the trip, even the part where he sent a two-man detail for the time she was there as an added protection. Only this time, something went wrong. Terribly, terribly wrong.

Sarge had planned the travel making it impossible to tamper with the arrangements unless someone close to dad or the benevolent society had tampered with the itinerary. Maybe it was one of her friends or the university staff, but she didn't share the trip's details, so that must rule them out. Besides, why would they? Robbie made the reservations and coordinated her cousin Gunner and brother Taren's trip as well.

She observed her captors individually. None of them looked well educated, no surprise there, but their levels of intelligence shown through. They were cautious. One man, Ahmed, seemed angry. He looked at the women with disdain, especially her and Maeve. That made him dangerous. She kept her eye on him. The second, Magan, was a risk-taker, making him a hazard of another sort. He didn't seem worried about the consequences of discovery, only at not getting his turn at the women. His hands were always touching or trying to molest when the other men weren't looking.

The third man, Cumar, was the leader. He spoke little, he made no eye contact, and his words cut sharply. His accomplices seemed eager to comply with his orders. He was simply mean; wolverine mean. Kayla had no wish to tangle with his demons. He walked ahead of the group, and that meant she always knew where he was.

She looked at the women around her as the words of her siblings came back to her.

"Kayla, do what you can for those around you, but when it comes down to it, you have to save yourself first before you can be of any use to others. Remember the airline attendant, 'don your mask first before assisting others.' Do that when you can't quickly gain control of the situation."

She centered her thinking. What were her assets? Her companions were holding up. They were getting some rest, and she was not hurt, well, she hurt, but she was okay for now. Kayla knew there was a time limit for that as well. *No, don't go there. Center. Identify your assets. Right.* Kayla could understand her captors' conversation well enough to get by; she had just relieved her bladder, so she was more comfortable, and she could run like hell if the need arose.

Kayla took a mental inventory of what remained in her hip pack after throwing out what they thought was important, like her camera and phone. She had a pen, floss, a small red marker, several socks and panties, a few toiletries, and a small bottle of sanitizer. In the corner of a side pocket that they had not searched were nail clippers and a metal nail file. Well, not too bad for an ambush. She wished she had her Go bag. But, then, that would be too easy.

The men seemed ill-prepared to kidnap them because they were whispering amongst themselves, and not watching their environment like this was their first rodeo. A rookie mistake they would have already paid for if she'd had better odds. A container of water dropped. Rosa stared at it as though it were a snake in a freshwater pond. If she reached to touch the water, the snake would strike. If she didn't try, she and the rest of her group would perish.

Kayla put her hand up to signal for Rosa to wait. Using her foot, she snagged the edge of the water bag and slowly dragged it toward them. The women carefully drank it between them. The plastic container was then replaced in a dark area on the ground so it wouldn't be seen. Before putting it in the hiding spot, Kayla placed her medallion ring inside. It had her initial on it. So, a message would be there if her spy party ever arrived and came looking in the right direction.

Kayla didn't have to alert the others when the men decided to move, the group of women had become hypervigilant, and for now, she counted that as another asset. As they walked, Kayla planned and watched everything she could. There had to be a way out of this mess. She didn't want to miss the opportunity if it presented.

They had changed directions slightly. Kayla used her nail file to shave the bark off the backside of a tree next to her, next made an arrow in the new direction with the small marker. It wasn't dark, nor large at all, so hopefully, she got her brother or someone like him to look for them. She was almost caught and thought it might be the last clue she could leave.

As the time crept on, her captors became less confident in their choices, stopping several times to argue about where they should go. Evidently, there were two places they could go, but the first one had too many people around and the second, further away. The silence and forever drudging through the desolate landscape made things nearly unbearable. And the thirst was never fully quenched. Even though they had shared the rather large water container, it wasn't enough. They had already begun to dehydrate.

Kayla's mind wandered. What would she miss in her life if she didn't survive this? Just that thought startled her with the reality of it. She had never paraglided or gone scuba diving. She hadn't ever had a child or gotten drunk. She'd never made love because she'd never been in love, was never engaged, never married, hell, not often interested in the men who came into her sphere, either. She liked guys; she just had never had more than sex with them. No lasting, romantic connections. She'd missed out on so many things.

She loved military men but would never commit to one because they all had issues, namely testosterone overload. She should know, she had enough of them in her life, but there had to be someone out there for her. When you get out of here, she told herself sternly, you are going to live a little, love a little, enjoy life a little more than you have allowed yourself thus far.

Kayla was deep in her thoughts when she walked into a spider web.

"Ahh," she said with a whole-body shiver. Her stomach roiled with the thought of a spider in her hair, on her face. She hated spiders. Detested them. She shook her body again, shoving her hand up to scrape the sticky intertwined silks from her face and hair, trying not to lose control of herself, more than she had. The desire was there, though. The men laughed at her as her companions helped to free her and check for insects while continuing their walk.

They continued their journey. Maeve was beginning to stumble even though they had recently had another rest. There were not enough of them, the water they shared, too little. They soon approached a clearing with a shabby shack, about the size of a fishing cabin, on a pond. It was surrounded by trash, old tin cans, and assorted other occupants' remnants. She listened to the conversation and heard enough to know they would stay there and wait for someone named Jamal. If they had the right cabin, that was.

She spoke in French to Maeve and Rosa, telling them what she knew. Thanks to her memory, high school French was good enough to communicate in a language the men couldn't understand. They didn't even clue in that the women were murmuring. When Rosa explained the situation to Sandraya, Ahmed told her to stop talking and knocked her to the ground. Sandraya stood frozen. Her eyes wide in terror, her body trembling. Rosa lay where she landed, whimpering and breathing heavily, but otherwise silent.

Their captors herded the women into the makeshift shelter, pushing and shoving roughly. Kayla tried to listen to what else was said, but the Somalians must have learned their lesson. Instead of talking of anything valuable that Kayla could use against them, the women were prodded and pushed into the filthy room filled with a wretched smell. Death. Kayla had to breathe through her mouth until she could deal with it. She wondered if the others understood the stench. Possibly Maeve did. She seemed very subdued. Or maybe, like everyone else, she was simply exhausted.

The door was kept open while their captors spoke outside. It helped in a small way to exchange the air. The next thing she knew, they were being crowded to a corner of the tiny room by the three men, joined by a fourth, Jamal. The door that had remained open to allow precious oxygen inside was closed. The men all turned to stare at the small group of women. Rosa began to sniffle.

The fourth man had broken teeth, yellowed by the lack of hygienic care, who spoke in equally broken English. "Who, Rhea? Who American?"

Chapter Three

River was restless, and like the rest of his team, he was ready to go, but it was too early. It had been some hours since the women had been literally snatched from the airport in broad daylight. River feared that the captors had assaulted the women by now, leaving them for the animals to devour. Another fate not easily explored was they might still be experiencing the horrors. That thought alone prevented him from falling into a deep restorative sleep. The operation's outcome appeared grim.

The alert call had come from the leader of the altruistic group that the women volunteered for, Mr. Sanchez. The leader and his male colleagues were unharmed except for the rebuffing of their ineffectual attempts to save the women. Something was off about this whole thing. It seemed as though it would have brought attention to the kidnapping. The recovery was River and his team's job now. It was Ms. Rhea's father's job to figure the rest out after his daughter's return.

Wide-awake as evening's darkness fell over the non-distinctive, rundown house they stayed in, River organized men who didn't need words to understand his thoughts. It was a skill working together as a team had given them. He'd miss it when he reentered the civilian world.

River gathered his gear, and the rest of the team did the same. Now, as they all fell back into active mission mode, they used hand signals and head movements to communicate. Like big cats, the men moved stealthily through the city, out to the camps that he suspected would be holding the women. It was mostly an unoccupied wasteland between where he was told the women had been dropped off and that shanty-town. It was a good place for a rendezvous.

Based on their intel, it was their best bet and likely their only chance at saving the women. While anyone could have kidnapped the small troupe, the male leader of their benevolent group had been obser-vant, if not a great protector. He gave River's Command the informa-tion they needed to be direct in their approach to the situation. Intel told them what direction they were going and that the group had been seen from the air before disappearing from view. River and his guys had to rely on knowledge of the area, the type of person who did these acts, their experience, and their instincts.

River expected the women, if alive, would likely have experienced beatings and been raped at least once by now. He wondered if Sergeant Rhea understood that. River shook his head and cleared it of other thoughts. His mission, his last mission, was to gain entrance, rescue the victims, and get the hell out of Dodge or, in this instance, off African soil.

They made their way to the camp that most likely held the captives. The area appeared to be operating as usual. That wasn't a tell, but there was usually a hut or something that more people were guarding or standing around. That did not seem to be the case here. He hoped that didn't mean there was no one to guard. River spread his men out.

Each man pegged which hostage was theirs to care for. He would snatch Rhea's daughter and pray he didn't gain a sobbing mess in the process. Civilians were always a wild card when it came to recovery. It certainly would be understood but not advantageous to their escape. The removal would be more difficult and bloody the more noise they made. He hunkered down to wait and watch for the right time to move. The bandana he used to stop the sweat from rolling into his eyes didn't halt the itch. He ignored the slickness on his skin and the insects at-tracted to it while he focused on his mission.

Grady and then Jonas motioned to the other side of the camp. They moved in that direction. A small ruckus at the far side of the encampment drew the team there.

"What did you find out?" asked Martine.

Jonas whispered. "Someone was talking about getting the American woman. They pointed in this direction. I figured it meant we have little time to find and extract."

River hoped like hell they made it in time. If the kidnappers were still on the other side of the small village, there would be enough time to find the women and get them out before shit hit the fan. Going over the plan, playing out different scenarios, or making a change was no longer an option. They continued to travel in the indicated direction, praying they found the women still alive. The voices River had hoped to hear was absent. If Martine had not overheard the conversation, River would have thought them at the wrong spot until female sounds alerted them that they were in the right place. Thank God. They needed to wait but not too long. He expected someone to exit the hovel.

The targets appeared soon after a ruckus in the hut directly in his line of vision. He watched the insurgents, just a ragtag group of male villagers and military wannabes, push three women out of the enclosure made of dried brush and discarded wood pieces tied with a wire that surrounded the little hut. It looked like that was all there were, three women. Two were young but didn't fit the description he had or that he remembered of Kayla. The young daughter of Sergeant Rhea was not there. Kayla Rhea's age made her a prime target to slake these men's sexual desires, but in River's experience, any woman would do.

Fucking hell that complicated this rescue immeasurably. River looked around to catch what the men were saying but couldn't make it out. The team needed to be closer, but that wasn't going to happen until they were assured they could keep the women safe, and not until he could make for damn sure Kayla Rhea was not still close at hand. The possibilities were grim. He pushed away all defeatist thoughts because even though he was irritated, these women were in the country; he had to hand it to them. They had a purpose, a calling, and didn't deter from their chosen path. However, this path had turned very dangerous. He wished he could lay his hand on a breathing Kayla to reassure him of her safety. The rest would work itself out.

River wondered if the young woman had been mortally wounded earlier and been tossed on the side of the road somewhere to die. On second thought, it was unlikely because they hadn't seen evidence of it on their way out here, and he was sure they followed the same general route. She had been smart. They had found a water container with her signet ring in it, showing the women had gone that way. Then he found a little mark on the scraped off bark of a tree indicating direction. There were plenty of broken branches and clues along the way to show the path of the small group's course. They wouldn't have missed her.

River watched his men as they spread out to cover the area better for a clean strike. Something wasn't right. The men weren't guarding them like they were assets to sell. The group acted as though they were waiting for something or someone. Dare he hope their contact was late or, even better, not coming? Or were they waiting on the women's rescue?

River began to focus his thoughts on the remaining women, watching their movements, their faces, the way they tried to look back at the little shack. No, that woman was close. He was about to signal to his team when an angry female voice spoke in an African dialect, Swahili. The American overtones were obvious. In response to her, harsh words were shouted, and a loud slap resonated in the space separating River from the incident.

Jerking his head to the side, he watched as the dirty, sweaty woman stumbled out of the little hut and fought with her captor. River grimaced as he saw her head snap back when the man yanked her long blonde hair. That woman would be Kayla Rhea. His chest tightened. She was grimy and beautiful, and she made his damn dick twitch. He caught himself before he charged in.to protect her. *You know better, Bennett.* He had rarely had to restrain himself, but seeing her, his body seemed to supersede his brain.

Damn, but she spouted her anger fiercely, and in a language that River was sure her captor understood. The Major appreciated she would be scared out of her mind. Still, he watched her as she used well-known kickboxing techniques taught to military personnel combined with some solid self-defense moves that only came to mind after hours of practice. His estimation of her rose exponentially when he saw her foot make contact with a rib. The man dropped like a stone.

He also understood that spunky women excited some men. Hell, they excited him but not at a time when his life balanced tenuously while trying to save hers. And not when his men would be clenching their teeth to hold their position after seeing the abuse she endured. He watched as her head bounced back again from the strength of the second slap to quiet her. River's fists tightened as he forcibly held his own position. She was a tough girl, and she would survive a few minutes more.

His first instinct included killing the man touching her, hurting her. His second was to hold her to himself. First, he wanted to kiss that lush mouth of hers, red from the slaps. Next, he would take care of her cuts and scrapes. He maintained his position while she was restrained. He looked to make sure the others were still ambulatory. It would make it easier.

He gave the signal once the women were left inside the hut. They were far enough on the edge of the little community that no one would notice. All, that is, except for the loud one. Kayla sat outside, hands and feet pegged together on the ground. River held an appreciation for her captors. It would be his choice of placement for her if the situations were reversed. Now it only complicated things when he needed to rescue her. She was a sitting target, out in plain view.

He moved in and prayed none of the women screamed or gave them away. It could become a blood bath if their instincts weren't strong and their experience wide. River thought only of his responsibility in the liberation, each slipping in and taking one woman at a time as assigned.

Finally, all three in the tent were out of the camp proper. The smoke from nearby cooking fires assisted the team as they slipped away unnoticed. As prearranged, they were on their way to the meeting place, ready for the extraction. Now it was River's turn to grab Kayla. She seemed to be working on separating herself from the stake in the ground when he slid inside the tent. Grady's precise cut in the back of the tent worked perfectly. River stealthily made his way to the front flap of canvas used as a makeshift door.

His voice sounded raspy, likely due to the adrenaline and the length of time he had remained quiet. His words came out of his over-dry throat in a harsh whisper, harder than he intended.

"U.S. military. Don't scream."

The girl, mercifully, responded as the others had done before her and stayed silent.

"I'm going to slip my hand out with a knife and cut your bonds, but you must remain still and not give us away. Move your finger if you understand."

To River's relief, the finger moved up and down twice, giving him the all-clear to slice her restraints. Once he had finished, her shoulders dropped to a more relaxed state. He slipped the blade back into his boot and listened before speaking. Kayla seemed to sense that silence was her friend right now.

"I'm going to slide you back into the tent and take you out the back exit we cut, so try to let me do the moving. Carefully look and tell me if anyone is watching you. Put up one finger if no, two if yes."

It seemed to take long minutes, but he knew time was relative in this situation. He kept his eyes trained on the woman's hands. One finger.

"Okay, now on three, you're going to be grabbed by me, and we will be gone. Don't fight me, just go with me. Can you run?" Two fingers. Yes.

"One, two..." he took her quickly to the back of the tent, then handed her out into his remaining teammate's grasp. Slipping out a second behind her, ready to cover their escape if needed, he followed Jonas into the surrounding vegetation. It all took less than a minute.

"Run!" came River's urgent whisper as he half scooped, half carried her to run at his speed.

He needn't have bothered. The girl was hurting, he could tell as her gait came down heavier on her left side, but she didn't slow her pace. He saw her grim determination, jaw taut, and he knew she was tough. And damn, he liked that in a woman. She wouldn't break in his hands if he took her hard and fast against a wall. His brain did nothing more than allow the thought to slide through his cognition and dissipate.

River nodded to Jonas, who took the lead, and River positioned Kayla between them before bringing up the rear. Running behind her, he could see she was near exhaustion, but they couldn't stop. Not yet. He continued to listen for the outrage in the camp but never heard it. No one was following. Good but suspicious. After traveling rapidly for about a mile, the girl tripped. She made only a grunting sound as she landed. She was stoic, but enough was enough. She would be unable to walk at all if they kept up the pace.

Kayla Rhea was the best kind of person to work in a situation such as this. As irritated as he was initially, he knew he had misjudged this woman. Mostly. She still had gone into a sizzling area of murders and chaos without an entourage of protection. He imagined the other women saw her as the real protection for their little group. Pathetic but not a bad choice if the truth were told. She held her own, and while she hadn't said a word, she was beginning to show real fatigue.

River spoke low. "You okay? We can slow down if you need to. We don't need to run full out now. We're nearly caught up to the others. You're in shape, and it helps." He helped her to stand and put four ibuprofen tablets in her hand, simultaneously reaching for his water container with his right hand. He offered it, as well. She took both.

"Drink slowly."

She nodded and took two slow swigs and offered it back to him. Kayla swiped at the assorted pieces of nature that were stuck to her sweaty body. "River? You are who you said you were."

"Yes, I have a habit of not joking around about things like that. Didn't you believe me?"

She shrugged and gave him a smile that lit up her face, making the dirt and swelling face insignificant to the sparkle in her eyes. She still took his breath away.

"We need to get you to safety, but I don't want to push you too hard."

Kayla nodded. "Thanks, but I can go further. I'd rather finish than rest too much. It will make it that much harder to start again. How far do we need to go?"

He took the jug back and took a swig himself, wiped his mouth, then stared into her wary eyes. Sweat rolled down her forehead and dripped onto her face, interfering with her sight momentarily. She blinked then squinted as she wiped her face with the bottom of her filthy tee shirt and swatted mosquitoes. River reached down and pulled another bandana from one of his many pockets.

"Hold on. I can help with that problem, at least."

Still keeping his eyes fixed on hers, he ran the cloth over her mouth that had started to trickle blood again. His gut knotted as he noted a harlequin of bruising under her tan. He tied the bandana around her head, smoothing her hair and rubbing his grimy thumb over her mouth. He answered her question, still holding her gaze. Her eyes never dropped once. He had a job to do. Get in. Get out. Deliver the package. Go home. He wondered what the chances were that he could take her home too? His home. *Back to business, soldier.*

"About three klicks. Another—"

"Couple of miles. Let's do it then."

He nodded and then broke the connection. Reaching down to assist her up, Kayla stared at his offering as though it were a cobra waiting to strike. Again, he connected with her eyes, briefly this time. She nodded and reached for his outstretched hand to accept his assistance. He pulled her into his arms and then swiftly released her, but it was too late. That lightning streak of arousal had already hit its mark, and his dick throbbed. His heart pounded. She felt it as well if her dilated pupils told anything. Her tongue came out to sail across her lips, nervously. He nearly lost his balance with her swift shove to push him away, causing him to release her immediately, only to instantly reach out again to support her suddenly unsteady legs.

He needed his head examined for playing with this little she-cat that hissed and purred in the same breath. Her expression said she didn't trust any man, and yet she had that undeniable attraction to him as well. This woman was out of his league. He had a long line of soft, pliant and *compliant* women just waiting in the wings for an offer to spend one night with him in vain hopes of two. Kayla was obviously neither waiting nor wanting, and yet, he wanted her more than the others.

He didn't know why, but he craved to sink into her in the worst way. And damn if River didn't want much more with her, even if he wasn't sure he was capable of more. He would be willing to try with a woman like her. Her family, knowing what baggage a hardened soldier carried with him, would discourage the connection, with good reason. After this week, he wasn't sure Kayla wouldn't need a luggage set of her own to deal with this experience.

They continued on, him in the rear, Martine forging ahead, and Kayla sandwiched between with no words exchanged until they arrived where the others were taking a break. These women seemed to have less stamina than Kayla. While his girl was more battered, the other three looked more devastated.

River turned away to say something to Martine, and he felt Kayla move toward the other women. He put pressure on the small of her back, his body reacting in an unconscious attempt to protect her even here with his team. She hesitated. That was a good sign that she understood his message. He rubbed his hand in a circular motion a few times before sliding it away. Again, she hesitated and even cut her eyes in his direction only to quickly shift them away and walk to the women. Her rejection and acceptance were communicated. His cock twitched.

Katz watched River and Kayla with interest. "Something wrong?"

River shook his head. "Not unless we don't get the hell out of here. I'm tired, hungry, and want my bed." Katz nodded in Kayla's direction. Katz chuckled quietly. "You're to the whining stage. Got it."

"Fuck off."

Katz nodded in the women's direction. "What's up with you two?"

"Nothing."

Katz cocked his head, "as in nothing you want to say or admit to, or nothing, nothing?"

"Come on. Let's go."

"Got it."

River took a deep breath and let it out slowly while rubbing the back of his neck. He knew the team could read each other pretty well, and Katz was better than most at deciphering unspoken truths, but dammit if he didn't even know what was going on himself. He was bone-weary and feeling it now that they were only a few miles from their transport out of here. That short-timer's syndrome was suddenly eating away at his psyche. That shit had to stop. He was on a damn mission.

Each member with a woman to protect took up their charge, leaving River to take over his. He felt his gut clench again, and his insides quiver with need. He slid his hand to the small of Kayla's back and propelled her forward. He'd evidently done it a little too roughly because her head twisted around to display a scowl.

When he raised his hands in surrender, her eyes, an unusual blue, sparkled, and she allowed a tiny movement of her lip. It was minute, but he saw it.

River relaxed. "Sorry."

She nodded, and he indicated that she continued walking. She did.

River appreciated her military family background. There was no complaint, no argument, just determination to get the task accomplished. She fascinated him. He liked how she was walking beside them or ahead of the other women, Maeve, Sandraya, and Rosa. Kayla was quick to give encouragement even though he could see what it cost her to do so. River felt that like him, Kayla's concentration on the others took away from her yearning to be done with this mission; to be home, to rest. And it kept River's impatience in check when one of the women, the youngest one, seemed to lag behind the others.

He gave Grady a look, and his team mate slid in beside Rosa to offer assistance. Kayla immediately looked up, and River saw her defensiveness. She was protective. She would be an incredible mother. Where the hell did that thought come from? He slowed his step until they were side by side.

"Grady will help her finish out the walk. We don't have far to go."

River didn't want to think about what might have happened to the women between kidnapping and rescue. The way Kayla coddled Sandraya and Rosa, he imagined it wasn't pretty. Maeve was stoic, but obviously, this had taken an enormous toll on her as well. These women had every right to whatever feelings they were experiencing. They had been gone less than two days, but that was more than enough time to wreak all sorts of havoc and destruction on them.

Pushing aside all thoughts other than getting to the extraction point, he nodded as Kayla looked over at him with a slight smile after leaving Grady with Rosa. Katz had partnered up with Maeve and Martine with Sandraya. In near silence, they accomplished the rest of the trip.

Chapter Four

Kayla looked over at Maeve and the other two women. Maeve, originally from Wales, lived in France now for her government job. Sandraya, from Brazil, and Rosa from Peru, were sheltered young women from well to do families who had battled with their families, as did Kayla, to come. Each woman was so different, but Kayla would always remember them with tenderness. They experienced something she had prepared for but had never expected to happen right off the airplane, even before traveling to the site. It took her unawares, and that was her mistake. And it became glaringly obvious the kidnappers knew Kayla's group was arriving on that flight.

Someone was waiting at the rendezvous spot to escort the three women to their embassies and home. Their goodbyes were tearful, but Kayla wouldn't let them see her lose the little control she had left and turn into a blubbering fool. As though sensing Kayla had hit her limit, River placed a steadying hand on her back. Nothing more was needed. She sucked in a ragged breath and made sure the women had her contact information and she, theirs before turning resolutely to face the team that had saved their lives. She had no doubt it was because of her family's ties to the military that she was going home with River's men rather than being dropped off at the U.S. embassy.

She knew her body stance had stiffened, and her face hardened, but she needed to keep it together. She tried her best to separate emotionally from the others. A survival technique that her dad and brothers had implemented often. They taught her well, but at what price? Was it practical to rein in her emotions so tightly that she was stone, or was it destructive? She hadn't the energy to figure it out.

Once inside, Kayla took stock of her surroundings. She noted the bathroom, which she used, the equipment already stored neatly, including their small returning arsenal of deadly weapons, and dropped into the seat indicated. River frowned. He seemed to be perusing his environment like he was seeing it for the first time. The interior was bare-bones, but it was a good transport, one she wouldn't have complained about regardless of the lack of comfort, but it was not an airliner, that was for sure.

"Okay, Peckerwoods." There was a pause. "Apologies to the lady present. Gentlemen, time to fly the unfriendly skies. Buckle up, Buttercups," came over the intercom, followed by an attempted demonic laugh.

"Hey, I'm Latino, you fu.." Martine stopped his response to the pilot. "Sorry, ma'am."

"Then he wasn't talking to you... this time." Katz shoved Martine good-naturedly, and they all laughed.

"Now, I'm being left out, segregated."

"Shut up. You don't know if you want to be included or excluded," said Grady as he ran his hand through his almost non-existent hair.

"You're cranky today, dear," teased Jonas.

Martine grinned and let fly. "Fuck off."

"Hey, stand down. We have a lady present." thundered River.

"Oh, hell, I'm sorry!"

The guys laughed. "Take a nap, Martine."

"Thanks, I think I will."

"Don't worry about me, guys. I grew up in a house full of military standards. I've heard worse."

"Still, I am sorry, ma'am," said Martine.

"Thank you, and it's Kayla."

Martine nodded in acknowledgment before he leaned back in his seat and closed his eyes. Katz glanced over at River, who was visually checking Kayla out. River shifted positions and caught him. Katz raised his brows in question. River knew giving her the once over visually was a fast way of seeing if she sustained any injury that she needed to be cleaned, but he was also enjoying the scenery.

"Need me to do a once over?" said Katz in his medic capacity. His question told River that they all considered Kayla under his personal care. Any other time that would have irritated him, but with Kayla, it gave him a feeling of rightness.

River turned to ask Kayla and saw she was fast asleep. Probably the first safe sleep she'd had since leaving home. That thought led to the belief that she should never have been in that situation. Which, in turn, brought him back to wanting to swat her behind for boarding without protection and then wrap her in his protection. And that fucking scared him.

"I think we're good until she wakes up. No seeping blood anywhere."

"There are a few cuts I see from here that we will need to clean as soon as, though."

"I'd noticed, but sleep will be good for her. Thanks, I'll get you when she's had a few hours."

He needed a little shut-eye too. They all did. After finding everything as it should be, he waited for the all-clear, the plane to taxi down the short runway, and finally go wheels up. They took to the air. Seeing she was sound asleep but unconsciously trying to find a comfortable position, River laid out his sleeping bag. Seeing Kayla had one attached to her backpack, he grabbed it as well. The benevolent group had saved her pack from the airport debacle, shoving it at one of his guys as they boarded. For a brief moment, he wondered why they didn't just hand it over to Kayla. He unbuckled her, picked her up, and settled her beside him to sleep on his bag, covered with hers. He tried to ignore the feeling of rightness he had doing it.

After Kayla had gotten a few hours of sleep, River woke her up.

"Hey, sleepyhead. Time to wake up. We need to clean your cuts up."

He cringed as he looked at her face, seeing the discoloration and swelling. It was worse than when they had found them. Likely to get even more colorful before it was over. Her look of immediate wariness followed by sitting up quickly seemed partly from disorientation to her environment and partly due to her experience over the last few days. He sat and waited for her to get her bearings.

"Hey, sweetheart. You're safe. You're with the River, going home."

She nodded and seemed to try to speak, but her mouth was dry, her lips chapped. "Water?"

"Yep. Gotcha some right here. Go slow, but drink it all if you can."

Kayla showed no signs of any difficulty swallowing down the whole bottle. Good. Now some electrolytes. She frowned.

"Too salty."

He sighed. Unfortunately, it wasn't an option. "Two large swigs for now." She hesitated. "Not an option."

She nodded and took a decent swallow that she accompanied with a grimace. "Good girl. That will help with the foggy brain. One more." Another pause and she took one last drink. He smiled as she shivered her distaste.

"How did you know?"

"Been there often."

"Yeah, I bet." She started to stand up.

"Hold tight. I want Katz to look you over first."

"Here?" Kayla looked around and saw the others were sleeping. She nodded. "Okay."

"Good girl."

Kayla's demeanor seemed to soften and then stiffen. "I'm a woman, you know."

It took a minute to sink in. River grinned and shrugged. "Oh, you certainly are, but "good woman" just doesn't seem to appeal in the same way as "good girl." You know?" She sniffed her disapproval, but he caught the tiniest of twinges at the corner of her lips. Good enough.

Katz took up a position next to Kayla with a medical kit. "Tell me what hurts. Where you know that there are wounds that need cleaning and dressing."

At first, it was fairly straightforward. She showed him her scratches and cuts. Katz addressed them. Then Katz asked to lift her shirt. "Um, sure." But the hesitation was there. Misreading her reluctance, River said, "I'll give you as much privacy as I can."

Her hand was on his thigh. "No." She withdrew her touch immediately. "I mean. You don't have to. I wear bikinis, so not much others haven't already seen." She was flippant, but he heard the insecurity. And damn if the statement that others had seen her partially undressed didn't rile him up. Unreasonable, but there it was. Hell, when was this plane going to land?

"Okay, sweetheart. I'll stay." She nodded and then bit her lip as she removed her shirt gingerly.

Her tan bra fit well, complimenting her skin tone. The angry red, black, and purple did not. River's swift intake of breath must have startled Kayla because she struggled, trying to replace her shirt. Katz shot him a frustrated look.

"No, hon. I'm sorry. I didn't realize you were so bruised. Honestly, it's okay. How much do you hurt?"

She bit her lip. "Some. I've had worse."

Katz said, "What?"

"When?" demanded River.

Kayla relaxed and almost giggled. "Brothers, remember?"

Both men sighed. "If you were mine, that would never happen again, even when horsing around."

She shrugged and sighed. "They are usually too busy now. We've all grown up. But when I was a kid, my brothers gave me almost anything I wanted after rough-housing with them. Otherwise, I'd show Sarge my battle scars. Dad said girls shouldn't have battle scars."

"Well, he's going to love the effects of this little misadventure."

He couldn't keep the approval of the Sgt Major's thinking, or his censure, from his tone. She had the grace to blush hard and look chastised. God, he just wanted to kiss her hard, spank her harder, and make fierce love to her. Hot, sweaty... Damn. She was staring at him, eyes wide, lip between her teeth. Siren.

Katz cleared his throat. "Right. Now take it all the way off so I can make sure I catalog all your war wounds." That had her laughing, and the moment was over.

No cracked ribs, but they were well and truly bruised. Her kidney had taken a hit, but Katz didn't think there was any internal bleeding. "The hospital will need to run a scan to make sure you aren't more than bruised. Even then, that is enough to stop any activities other than daily needs for several weeks. You get me?"

"Yes, sir."

Her first 'yes sir' and Katz got it? River caught himself. *And you don't care, soldier. Much.*

"You're a lucky little girl because if I had my way, you would be displaying that pale bottom for some up close and personal attention."

"That seems unfair." She shook her head. "No, it *is* unfair."

"Why did you leave if your detail wasn't with you when you boarded?"

"Because they are usually a step ahead of me. I arrive in-country and they're waiting for me to deplane. No one was there this time."

"When you realized your protection was not with you, you should have called home immediately."

"I did."

"And?"

"And nothing. I told Sarge, and he got immediately angry. Then frantic. If you know my father, then that is a statement all by itself. He told me to go to a certain hotel, but as you know, I never made it. I'm sure he hasn't quit raging. Oh," her eyes widened, "I didn't tell him I was okay."

"The pilot radioed Command. I'm sure they called your father."

"I'm assuming he threw someone on a plane that he would have to get back home, now."

"Likely after they do some checking around."

"No doubt. I figured Sarge would call in the Army. I was right." She made a gesture to reference the plane and the inhabitants inside. "My cousin or brother or another like-type person is probably doing that follow-up sweep of the incident. I'll get read the riot act, and then life will go back to normal."

"Except it won't for a while."

She raised mournful eyes to River's. "I know."

Katz patted her knee and stood. "Good as it's going to get until you get to a hospital." He packed his remaining gear in his kit and turned to help her up. River had already scooped Kayla up and held her steady as she got her bearings.

"I'm fine. I won't need a hospital. Nothing broken, nothing out of place. Scratches and the rest will heal without assistance."

"Except you could have a bleed. I don't think you do because while your belly is bruised, there aren't any other signs that there is a build-up." Katz's face relaxed.

"See, fine."

"Nonetheless, you will go. It's procedure." Katz put on his bossy voice.

Kayla laughed, but it had little mirth. "Sure thing. But if I'm good, there is no need to go. If I don't feel any worse than now, internally, by the time we land, I imagine that will prove I don't have a bleed."

River watched Katz turn to move away. River's arm came around Kayla's upper belly carefully to hold her in place. Before she could say or do anything, he landed a hard, fast kiss followed by a swat on her ass.

"Ouch. Feel better now?" she asked in a breathy whisper.

He leaned into her, speaking close to her ear. "Yes, actually. I've wanted to do that for hours. You will follow orders, little girl. I expect to hear you saw a doctor then followed his orders as well. Understood?" She nodded. "I need to hear the words."

"Yes, sir." She dipped her head and then raise up to give him a saucy wink.

He kissed her cheek. "I like hearing that from you." He caught her look of vulnerability and something else. Arousal? Longing? It made him want to wrap her up in bubble wrap and take her home.

On the rest of the flight home, his estimation of this woman rose even higher.

"An escort was Dad's idea. But I didn't know they had the wrong date until I had the confirmation of a change. It didn't seem like much, a few hours, but it meant the whole itinerary was completely different. They were to come in nearly a whole day later, then my trip was changed again without my knowledge, at the airport. Once dad fixed it, the dye was cast. I know this was intentional. It was too easy. I just don't know why."

The surge of protective feelings he felt towards Kayla was a surprise. Whether pleasant or not, it wasn't easy to determine at this stage. He'd not felt this way about another woman unrelated to him. Hell, he didn't feel it about any woman except his sister, and that hadn't happened since her marriage to another military man. He defended women and men alike, but this left an ache in his midsection that moved to his cock. Yeah, just lust, surely. His brain berated his avoidance of the issue, but what could he do? He couldn't act on it. Not now.

She was the daughter of a man who, by reputation anyway, ate tough soldiers for breakfast. Kayla never asked for River's care nor did anything to give him the impression she needed it, but she didn't repel it. After that one emotional moment of weakness, she was holding onto them tightly. She'd obviously learned to handle life herself.

In short, she was exactly as the only daughter of a command sergeant major should be: self-sufficient, confident, and appreciative. Unfortunately, she was also intelligent, single, and attractive. In River's estimation, those things were not an asset in this environment; they made her bait. The thought of someone using her as a lure to entice others into their lair or induce them to do something in exchange for time with Kayla made him sick. He had no doubt it was just what her captors would have done. They would have sold her to the highest bidder and let her be theirs to use and abuse. He had no doubt the kidnappers would have had a go at her before turning her over.

That scene flashed across his mind's eye, leaving a distinctively uneasy feeling, unsettling his gut, enraging him. He had to let it all go. His libido and machoism needed to stand down. He took a step back from her, she shivered, he inhaled deeply. Pull it together, man. You can do what she needs and walk away.

River watched as Kayla thanked each of his men individually and chatted with them briefly before returning to sit next to him for the remainder of the flight home. She had worn herself out again. He bit his tongue when he saw she was moving more slowly. Her adrenaline had leached out, leaving her even more fatigued than when they'd finally stopped running. He wanted to take care of her as much as he had hoped they wouldn't interact again.

Kayla sighed and relaxed her muscles. She slumped in her seat, leaning on him, her weariness evident. Even in her exhaustion, she seemed to want to engage River, and he obliged. Sleep was overrated.

"Tell me about your family."

"Well, let's see. I've got one sister. My parents wanted me in the business they have been running their whole adult lives, and I rebelled."

"Because you don't want to go into the family business."

"I do, and I will soon, but I didn't want to do it without examining the world from a different set of lenses."

She snuggled closer. "I understand that completely. When I go on benevolent ventures, I tell my story in pictures."

"How long have you put yourself in danger to take some pictures?"

Anger rushed to the surface. "That's not what I'm doing," she said vehemently. Her voice lowered, but the passion never lessened. "I work with the young girls that are stolen from their families and tormented by ruthless men. When those arrogant bastards are done, the horrors aren't over because the girls' families won't take them back. No one will marry them, not that they are interested in that after what they have endured. They are left destitute to starve or be killed by marauding animals. They often make money by getting into a larger town and exchange sex for food and a place to live."

River patted her hand. Kayla yanked it back. "Hey, I'm not patronizing you. I'm trying to give a little comfort without drawing attention."

Kayla took a deep, shaky breath. "Thank you. I'm sick to death of people thinking I go for the thrill. Believe me, there is no thrill when you see what a young girl looks like after returning or how she reacts when she isn't received back into the family. We've set up a home for these girls in an area some distance away but still close enough. If a parent is ill or something happens, she can get back and forth."

"And is this place successful?"

"Sure, well, most of them are. I mean, we dig a well, supply food and seeds to plant. The only meat is what they can hunt. It's not a reliable source, so we make sure they have protein in the beans they grow and chickens for eggs. When they quit laying, they eat the chicken."

"And so, you take pictures of this whole thing?"

"Yep. I have taken pictures of all kinds of things."

"And you show the world?"

"Yes. Two years ago, my photo journal was picked up and added to an international story about this same issue worldwide. It comes in different colors and different shapes and sizes, but it is definitely a universal horror."

"Were these photos of the men who kidnapped girls?"

"Yes. I don't censor anything."

"Then I would lay odds, that's why you were followed, tracked to the airport, and snatched. I imagine they want to silence you. They must have done a lot of background work to orchestrate all of this. Now that they have lost you after all their efforts, I imagine that won't be the end of it. If you return to Africa, you will likely be killed."

Kayla was subdued when she next spoke. "I wondered about that. What else can I do? It's my calling to help these girls."

"Then let's look at it another way. We have a Foundation gala later this year. Would you be willing to tell your story? I'm sure it would gain you some contributors for the cause, and then you use that money to help them instead of showing up in person. Win-win."

"It sounds amazing. Can I think about it?"

"Of course." He pulled her close again and sighed heavily while covering a big yawn. She grinned sheepishly. "Sorry. You must be dead on your feet. I can't imagine how wiped you feel after a mission."

"I'm soon to retire. I figure it's about time to find out what life would be like without living on snatches of sleep amongst bugs, heat, and languages other than English. I've always spent my down-time in my home, if possible. It's a short flight from Seattle to Port Refuge, and I take advantage of it."

"Is that where you grew up? Where is your family?" Her eyes widened as she realized how personal the question was. "Oh, sorry. You don't have to answer that."

He smiled. "I grew up partially on Cache Island, partially in Seattle. My parents have an Engineering Firm and a few other irons in the fire, including the family Foundation. The main offices are run out of Seattle because it needs to be, but the brains of the operations, my parents, live on Cache Island. As do I. My sister and her husband live closer to Tacoma."

"How about you? Does Sarge live in Seattle?"

"Yes, Lake Forest Park. You had an event there."

"I seem to remember that event. I bet, foundations don't warrant even a blip on your father's radar."

"I am my father's daughter, but he is not my owner. I do plenty of things outside of his realm." River heard the defensiveness.

"Sorry. I hope I'm not the only one to make that mistake."

After a second, she shook her head and gave him an indulgent grimace. "Unfortunately, no. But I want people to start treating me as a person outside of my father or my brothers."

"Which is what? A professor at the university?"

"No, and I don't want to be, either. I'm a media photographer, so teaching others about how photography is so much more than days at the beach and selfies, is my goal. I offer insight into journalistic photography, and so much more."

"I bet it's hard in this computer culture."

"The "it's all about me" group makes it more challenging, for sure. But the students that get it do well."

The longer they spoke about the issues of the day, and nothing of any importance, learning tidbit about themselves, River found that he liked her more and more. She had wit and was tenacious when she wanted something that ran against the grain for others. He enjoyed the feistiness, engaging her by taking the other side of an issue just to hear the delicious blonde defend her ideology.

They stayed away from the incident itself because his situation report needed to include his interpretation of events, and her debrief should cover only hers. He needed more sleep, and so did she, but his desire to spend every moment possible with her overrode his call to replenish. It commandeered his good sense. She laughed, and his gut seized. He fucking loved that sound. He'd move heaven and earth to hear it every day. When she finally dozed off again, he'd watched her for a while before catching a catnap himself, only to instinctively wake when she moved, then doze again to the soothing sound of her breathing and her hand on his thigh.

As the flight ended, they both gathered their gear and hesitated. Kayla seemed to be battling with herself over something. He fought his urge because unless fate brought them back together, this was the last he would see this interesting woman. They would debrief in different places and not cross paths again. He could look for her but he would be part of a memory she would want to be erased.

He watched her with surprise as she reached over and kissed him full on the mouth. Her hot breath and musky earthiness blended with her sweet sweat overwhelmed his senses and demanded his response. He didn't have a choice, her body called to his.

He tried to quickly find a reason to resist. Her fingers tightened around the front panels of the flak vest he'd put back on to exit the aircraft, pulling him closer with an insistent tug. His libido rose, his cock following the command. River answered her call and gave as good as he got until finally, she pulled away. Kayla was breathing harder than he was, but he felt the drain.

"Thanks for the rescue," she said huskily, "and the comfort, River. I won't ever forget you. You will always be my hero."

And he would never forget her. Kayla's lips were soft and pliable as they touched again, each drawing succor from the other, leaving him primed for the action of another primitive variety. As she stepped back from her kiss, he realized that he had been partially hard the whole flight back. Maybe since he laid eyes on the blonde beauty fighting her captors like a spitting cobra. Once his survival instincts stood 'at ease,' when he knew she was safe, another elemental drive, the lusting part of him, took over. He mentally chastised himself as she disembarked the plane. *You are too old for her, man, probably a decade, maybe more.*

River stood off to the side as his men were loaded into their transport and watched Kayla as she approached her father and two brothers. She pointed in his direction, waved, and then River watched the group approach him. The sergeant stopped at the military transport and said something to the driver, who nodded in response. Ronald Rhea joined his sons as they shook River's hand.

"Kayla says you are the leader of these men, and it was you who orchestrated her rescue. Son, I don't know who you are or what you plan to do in your life, but if you ever need someone at your back, you've got three. Hell, if you ever leave your present situation, I've got a job at your disposal. Taren," He indicated the taller and more muscular of the sons and River appreciated his firm grip when they shook hands.

"No words, Major. She's everything to us."

"I can see why. You might want to keep better tabs on her from now on, though."

"River!" complained Kayla, her hands planted firmly on her hips. Her face turning bright red.

Sarge raised his eyebrows. "Stand down, young lady. Adult or not, you're always my little girl. We will be discussing this mess."

Her demeanor changed. "Dad, I think it was a set-up."

Sarge nodded and pulled Kayla close. "We'll talk about it." His tone was strong enough to curb any response she was about to give.

With an answering nod, she leaned into her father's sturdy hold.

"And this one is my eldest, Rob. Best man on a computer system that I know."

Rob laughed. "He only knows me." He reached his hand forward. "Thanks, man. She can be a brat, but we love her and would have missed her." He ruffled her hair. "She's the glue that keeps us together, and she stops us from killing each other."

"You're more than welcome." He looked at his transport. "As much as I'd like to chat longer, I have some tired guys and a long day left."

Taren and Sarge saluted River, which he returned. Rob held out his hand, and Kayla hugged him one final time. Too quickly, they were gone. Kayla looked back once and waved until he returned the gesture. She wiped her eyes and was gone from his life. And what the hell was he going to do about that?

As River joined his team, he realized he hadn't given her his full name. If they had been in uniform, that would have been brandished across his chest, and he suddenly wished he had told her. His last mission, and he already felt he had unfinished business.

He hoped the more tangible pieces of the memory would eventually fade because he would endure a perpetual hard-on if it didn't. No, just six more months left in this man's army, and he'd be a civilian again. Kayla Rhea would move on with her life, as she should. As they both should.

Chapter Five

One Year Later

Kayla Rhea enjoyed her life. Most said she showed exceptional maturity for her age, which she translated to mean *dull*. The youngest child should make her the life of the party, but it didn't. Robbie was her parent by proxy when she was younger. He stepped in and took the place of both father and mother when her mother passed away. The tragedy left eight-year-old Kayla to grow up in an all-male household. Her father, Robert Rhea Sr., Sarge, had been active duty Army at the time with gone as much as he was home.

Kayla looked over at her father as he entered the kitchen, the picture of health and still commanding an army, only now it was a civilian one. She loved him something fierce, but she had missed a mother's influence. The military man said he wanted to devote more time to raising his daughter, and Kayla knew in her heart he did, but it didn't happen the way he or she had hoped.

Kayla tried to understand how difficult life was for Sergeant Rhea, who lost his wife of twenty years to a senseless diving accident. Then accepting the CSM because he needed to support his family, and Kayla suspected, keep busy. Meeting all the needs of an adolescent girl could be difficult without another female around. She had been happy enough, if somewhat overprotected.

"Hey, pumpkin. What's on the schedule for today?"

"No classes today, so I thought I'd clean my gear and check it."

"Going camping?"

"You could say that." She offered a sandwich to Sarge, which he accepted. She made herself another one.

Sergeant Rhea didn't retire until five years ago. He'd waited until Kayla graduated from college with a master's degree in International Media Relations, with a focus on journalism and photography. Quite by accident, because of her desire to help, she'd made a name for herself. Kayla Rhea wasn't always well received, but disagreement for her exposure of atrocities committed against poor African village girls was rare.

She had tried to go back on the next trip but found it was too soon after the kidnapping. Her family wasn't in favor of her going back at all. She recalled her father's words when she had suggested it.

"Kayla, honey, I understand your need to help. It's admirable. It's inspiring. But right now, it is also irresponsible and out of the question." His tone was well known to his children. It was the "no way in hell" tone.

"I appreciate your fear for me. I do. It's something that I have to do, dad. Yes, there's a danger. But someone needs to help those girls."

"Why do you have to be the one?"

"You didn't really mean that question, right? If not me, then who? You brought me up to care for my fellow man and, in this case, woman. I'm helping. When I get media coverage on this issue, I keep the world informed. I'm influencing something bigger than me. Isn't that what a productive citizen of the world tries to do?"

Sarge grimaced. Kayla had speared his objections with his own arrow. Not everyone agreed with her methods, but if she had to ruffle a few feathers to live according to her convictions, so be it. She wasn't in the habit of doing what other people told her to do, especially when what they wanted went against what she believed to be right. Her father had ultimately let the subject drop. Kayla knew that meant he was taking matters into his own hands, and so far, he hadn't crossed any lines. Except things had gone wrong the last time.

The boys did a brisk business with Sarge, who ran Rhea Defense and Security Agency full time now. Sergeant Rhea started as a consultant, a silent partner when Taren and his military buddies approached him. They were interested in trying their hand in the securities business, but Dad came with the connections. The longer experience, the reputation desired, and his need to stay busy also played an integral part.

"Hey, Lala peep-peep. How goes it?"

"Good, and stop calling me that." As a girl still feeling lost after her mother's death, she had been hesitant to take on new things, so her brothers had said she was a chicken. She was the baby, so... peep-peep. Lala was her toddler version of Kayla. The boys never let her forget.

Ever the computer geek, Robbie had his hands in more of the world's secrets than anyone suspected. He left the military intelligence after the start-up, but running the business would never be his forte. Taren was a boots on the ground operator, anxious for some fieldwork to tackle. Getting down and dirty is what made Taren happy. He wouldn't run the business. His buddies were cut from the same cloth.

That left Sarge to be the admin. He enjoyed running the show, passing out the assignments, doing sit-rep reviews, and holding the commander position second nature. Kayla loved that her dad continued to be so active in her brother's lives; however, there wasn't a spot for her in what was now the family business. Mafia-style.

"Can you make me one of those, *Kayla*?"

"This isn't 1950. Women do have lives, jobs, careers, ambitions, dreams..."

Robbie put his hand up. "Fine, I'll make my own sandwich."

"No, I don't mind making it. I just want to be appreciated."

Rob put his arms around Kayla and gave her a loud kiss on the cheek. "I always appreciate you." He was serious. She made his sandwich.

She realized the problem continued to be that she wasn't male. And because of that little unchangeable fact, the men in her life were overprotective. Kayla proved she had a sharp mind, a quick wit, and was physically fit, none of which her father or brothers paid attention to when it came to the division of labor. They offered her the position of office manager. She had no interest in sitting in an office and getting people coffee. She knew the job included more, much more, but it still came down to something she absolutely hated to do.

Kayla wanted to be part of the gang, part of the group, not left on the fringes. She recalled her most recent conversation with her father and brothers just yesterday.

"What are you up to today?" asked Sarge.

"Planning my next photo trip."

"Where to this time?"

"Same area as last time."

"It's too much of a hot spot, Kayla. You aren't going back there. It's more volatile than when you went a year ago. Gunn and his unit weren't there in time to rescue you, for God's sake. I never found out why you were compromised. You were scared to death; don't you remember? I nearly had a stroke worrying about you."

Oh, she remembered, all right. She remembered a certain, melt your panties, Major River. She'd been scared out of her mind, but River treated her with respect. He showed compassion, even though his assessment of the whole ordeal remained rough. After a few hours rest, he'd made sure she had no life-threatening injuries. Then he'd chastised her.

"What do you mean reckless? I followed the protocol and tried to be safe. I wasn't raped, not physically anyway. They did a number on my psyche, though. But I'm strong, and I'll be fine."

"A miracle you weren't raped, yes. You have plenty of bruises and cuts that are going to take a while to heal. But don't hold onto the thought you were spared physically because you were effective in rebuffing your abduc-

tor. If he'd wanted to take you, if any had, they would have gang-raped you if you were too hard to handle alone. Conscience would not be an issue for them. The bottom line is you knew it was dangerous, and you did it anyway. I'm telling you, don't ever do it again."

She wanted to shout, *I'm an adult, and it's what I can do to better the world.* And *what business is it of yours?* Instead, she held her tongue. He'd risked his life and the lives of others to get the women to safety. He didn't deserve her rant, but the silence had been deafening, and yet her ears were full of the beat of her heart as she sat scrunched up next to him. Damn it, she liked his take-charge attitude. By his mere presence alone, he'd helped her feel better, relaxed, more protected. After what she had just gone through, that was not to be taken lightly. She didn't.

Kayla loved how River's hand went around her shoulders to steady her when they hit turbulence. He did it again when she'd been too tired to stay awake, allowing her to cuddle tight as she slept. A piece of heaven she hadn't been able to erase. She didn't want to forget. Her father's insistent voice brought her back from her musings, causing an irrational, angry blip to flash across her mental radar.

Sarge reasoned, "A young woman who does free-lance writing and produces award-winning pictures should be able to find safer work and still get her message out."

"Dad, why do you think my work is desired so much? It is the subject matter, the realism. Besides, I do plenty of work during the year to finance my annual trip to Africa. It isn't as though I'm a daredevil looking for a thrill. Those girls and young women need what I can provide them, both physically and in the media. It brings money and awareness, and that's important."

She knew the trip also created a symbiotic relationship between her need to make a difference, the village girls affected, and the impact of her art. Her trips were a win-win.

"Until things are more settled, you aren't going back there. Find a new adventure."

She'd heard it all before, too many times to count. Even now, the 'laying down of the law' continued to be a common mantra in the Rhea household. Same song, different day. She'd learned long ago to tune the arbitrary edicts out. She was Sarge's only daughter, she got it, but it could get too much, quick. That's why she and Sarge split the rent on a small efficiency she maintained for her days when she needed to work, the house was too noisy, or the conversation too volatile. Like today.

Kayla taught adjunct at the local college part of the time. When she wasn't concentrating on women's issues in other countries, she wrote about current world events. She did seminars on various subjects, published articles, and displayed her pictures that told the girls' heartbreaking stories. Her popularity in the artistic and seminar realms had taken off in the last year. Her notoriety had risen ever since she'd published an article telling her pictorial story of a village in Somalia two years before. With her kidnapping a year ago, she had become what Taren called a "hot item."

Kayla did as she always did in these situations with the menfolk; she agreed, then went on to do what she wanted to do. This time she noticed her father was not as mollified as in her previous experiences. Kayla feared he'd figured out her stratagem. She would work on a new one after she got back from her next trip. Now it was time to organize the new expedition itinerary and set things up more quietly since her father forbade her to return to Somalia.

The final part of her latest work hadn't been accomplished since she was kidnapped and couldn't get to the village. She'd need to avoid the subject at home from now on and deflect any more conversation. Not a skill she had honed but, she would. It was that important.

It wasn't long after the year anniversary of her kidnapping that things really began to go south in a hurry. Taren had gotten wind of the official worries for her safety when he went to Somalia to help a diplomat out of a touchy situation. His contacts in the region told him of the whispers behind closed doors of a plan that included taking his sister. Those who were making money from human trafficking in the area wanted her work stopped.

Taren immediately sent the information home to Robbie, who investigated further. Kayla received yet another command to appear in her father's office. She was aware the timing was predictable. Once again, even though she'd waited another six months and didn't take Christmas break to visit the Congo for a week, that would not be enough concession for her family.

"Kayla, Taren will be here tomorrow, but he sent word to warn you. Your life is in danger. You cannot return to the same region you were in before. I know of other places you can go to for benevolent work. In fact, there is a good group anxious to get their story out. They're well protected, too."

"Dad, I haven't even sat down. What are you saying exactly?"

"You aren't to go back there. Taren says they are waiting for you. They want to get their hands on the 'woman who interferes' according to his sources."

"Dad, I'm not so well known that there would be an organized plot to kill me."

Robbie walked in the door carrying a deep frown on his face. "Or worse. Yes, Kayla, that is exactly what's going on. The next time you go to do your humanitarian work in that region, you will be a target. You do good work, sis, and you're beginning to gain notoriety."

"Kayla Rhea, I am not asking you this time, I am telling you, you can't go."

"Dad, I'm an adult."

"One that needs to become reacquainted with my knee,"

"Cute. You never laid a hand on me."

"Maybe I should have. Honey, I'm sorry, but you can't go back. Not now. What I can get behind is showing you a list of alternatives."

"Dad. Look, we've gone over this. I can do what I think is right without your permission."

Robbie interjected his own ammunition. "You know, I can get you on the no-fly list. It just takes a little work and to call in a few favors. I have a huge ledger of favors owed me." She had no doubt Robbie did.

"Can I think about your alternative offers? I wasn't ready to change direction yet, but give me the organizations' name, and I'll research them."

"Good, honey. I know you hate it, and so do I for you, but I would never forgive myself if I let you go where you were likely to be killed."

She did know, especially since she had gotten an email that morning from some lunatic that threatened her life. Or, rather, promised she would be unable to "interfere anywhere, ever again" if she went back to the village in Somalia. She could tell any of the men in her family, especially Robbie, and he would find out where it came from, but that would put paid to any travel plans she had until they found the crazy. She got random hate mail, but this one felt personal, specific.

They were wrong, she didn't want to die, but intimidation was a heavy weapon the world's bullies lived on. She'd put off her last trip for her family. River's words came back to haunt her, "You're reckless. The bottom line is that you realized the danger, and you did it anyway, putting everyone else's' life in danger to find you. Don't ever do it again."

Why did she give him so much space in her brain? Because she really liked him. Bossy butt and all.

She shivered now just as she had then. River had meant it. She should listen to everyone, find a new area to focus on, and play by the rules. However, Kayla being Kayla, standing up to opposition from the men in her family was a learned skill. She didn't obey orders very well. And, with her family's business, that was a problem.

Kayla knew slave trading and human trafficking permeated the free world as well, but plenty of people worked hard to stop it in those countries. She wanted to go somewhere others weren't already dealing heavily with the issues. She had let her father send protection the last two times, but it hadn't made a difference. Whoever wanted her had succeeded by knowing just what to do to get her.

Kayla's real problem had come in when she didn't tell her family she was going. Well, she had told them, but when she got the change at the airport, she assumed they had already known. They hadn't. Because of the abduction, the heightened dangers, she couldn't tell them when she went again. How could she? They would try to stop her, and they could, but she knew she couldn't let them.

The next week, Taren walked into the family home after the same tired conversation progressed from another round of the 'thou shalt not' to the more amiable topic of dinner.

"Hey, Lala, what's going on in your world?"

"Why can't you call me by my name or even Kayla like Robbie does?"

"Because you still call him Robbie, and you are still my baby sister."

"Okay, if I start calling him Rob, would you stop calling me Lala?"

Taren's muscles flexed as he tried to fold his arms. He was only partially successful in the attempt. Not for the first time, Kayla admired the man her brother had become. His military career had been an excellent experience for him. Still, she appreciated he kept many of the darkest times away from her. She caught her dad and Taren talking about it at night, but they would shut it all down when she came into the room, as though she hadn't seen her share of horrors. Taren didn't intimidate her when he had an opinion different than hers, much to his chagrin.

"Nah, don't think so, but Robbie might like it."

"Robbie might like what?" Out of the back of the house came the subject of the last statement.

Kayla rolled her eyes. "Oh, never mind. What do you want for dinner?"

Robbie treated her the same way as her Dad and Taren when disclosing information about his deep, and Kayla suspected, alarmingly dark, computer work. It didn't interest Kayla in the least all the sinister ins and outs of covert activity via the web. Whatever it involved, it had many interwoven tales of intrigue in the defense and security realm. Robbie was their ears to the ground, her dad said, and she didn't doubt it.

"Dad, you know, I could work up prospective clients for you, screen the inquiries, and either accept the job or refer them out."

"I do that already."

"Right, but I could free you up to do the operations side."

"I already do that too."

"But—"

"Kayla, I don't want you exposed to unsavory characters."

"Then I guess I should stay home and in my room. They're all around me," her sarcasm bounced off the walls.

"Now that's enough of that, young lady. Aren't you too old for a tantrum?"

"Ohh!" she made a quick exit before the conversation deteriorated further.

Kayla checked her inbox. In her personal account was a photo of one of the girls she'd helped. According to the email, the girl had been sold by a family member and now sighted in South America. The girl was not enjoying the weather but outside a whorehouse. Who had sent this to her? Probably someone at Hope That Matters.

She ran her mouse over the email address at the bottom and found a different address. Hmm, Robbie said that meant that the sender didn't want you to know who sent the message for whatever reason. Odd. This photo would segue nicely into her next area of work after the Africa trip, the exportation of women to bordellos without their consent. Wouldn't her family love to hear about that future direction?

Chapter Six

Jonathan River Bennett III, known as River to his friends and family, controlled a portion of his family's empire. He had plenty of friends and associates, yet, he was lonely. The few times he'd tried dating, were unfulfilling and it had been a long time since he'd warmed his bed with anything besides a blanket.

River was educated at a prestigious university earning an MBA with an emphasis on nonprofit and strategic administration. Figuring outcomes and planning for those was his strong suit making him prime real estate for CEO of Bennett Foundation. But, at the end of those accomplishments, he'd already felt trapped.

Before anyone realized it, he'd jumped the business ship and taken his twenty-fourth year to travel the world. At the end of that year, when his family took a collective sigh of relief, he joined the Army as a strategic officer. His mother cried, and his father remained strangely silent on the subject. River often wondered if his father envied his impulsivity and daring to go against family tradition and expectations to do what he wanted to do.

Being the strategic officer for extended campaigns and active missions, he honed his strengths as an intellect and military fighting machine. He'd enjoyed the challenge. And it had been good for a while, excellent, in fact. River enjoyed the strategizing and collaboration the missions always offered him. Still, by the end, the actual boots on the ground wore him out. The older he got, the more jobs he worked, both on the ground and in the Com Center, and the harder they were to recover from. The devastation was sometimes overwhelming.

He'd felt the continual responsibility for other soldiers' and civilians' lives with little break. It had ultimately been the wearing away of his mental outlook, his mind, body, and solid bits of his soul that made him decide to surrender his commission. He didn't want another military job, he wanted to go home. He'd served his country twelve years, doing recon intelligence for the last four years. When his final assignment ended, he gave it all up because he'd begun to dislike the man he faced in the mirror each morning. That person was harder, colder, and unforgiving. And alone.

The last mission came as a surprise he would never forget. He'd felt a strong affinity with Kayla Rhea. Now, after a year, he could function nearly a week without thinking about the blonde firecracker whose attitude melted, and her bravado disappeared when he had drawn her close after her ordeal. But she never surrendered ground she didn't want to, much like her father and her cousin, his friend, Gunther Rhea. The Sergeant's nephew affectionately and respectfully referred to as Ray Gunn or just Gunner. He ran into him just the other day.

"Hey, Gunner, how's your cousin these days?"

The men shook hands. "Which one?"

"Kayla."

"As insubordinate as ever, but she's gaining in popularity with her humanitarian work."

"I bet her dad spends all day keeping her in line."

"You'd think, but really, except for the stubbornness in doing riskier work than anyone thinks she's doing, or than she needs to be doing, she's a great girl. Besides, her brothers and dad started a new venture a few years back. They own and operate a security agency. They have a good handle on watching over her, you might say."

"So I heard."

"The old man runs the admin, Robbie is IT hanging out with dark web people, and his eldest, Taren, is using his spec ops training to work the ground."

"They do it all alone?"

"Nah, they handpick their own people, and I do mean, handpick. When I leave this hellhole, I'm going to work with them. Better pay and a different commitment because I'm doing what I believe in. You know, where we get to decline those missions not done for its moral rightness. In the military, we just do it because orders are orders. Sarge only does what he believes in."

"Sounds like heaven."

"Hey, when you separate out, give him a call. Hold on, here's his number. He would jump at a chance to sign you on."

"Been out six months. I do some fill-in training for Captain Zayden Wellesley near my home. He has this multi-agency, combined military training unit. He's a SEAL, all of his trainers are elite, and I hooked up with them before exiting. I keep my hand in with them when needed. Aside from that, I have family business obligations I am expected to meet. It does sound good, though. Maybe I'll talk to Zayden and see if there is room for collaborative efforts if Rhea is in agreement."

"Hey, I'd have never thought of that. I hope it works out."

"Thanks. I'll see how it goes."

Gunn obviously tossed his name out immediately, because two weeks to the day after they'd talked, came the call from Robert Rhea.

"Hey, I know this is intrusive as hell, but it's worth a shot. I spoke to my nephew, Gunner, and I know you just relinquished your commission this past year. I also hear you're working with Zayden at the training center near your home in Alaska. I wondered if you were interested in checking out my operation and maybe give me a hand now and then. Your knowledge and reputation precede you. Why don't you come in and let's chat?"

"I told Gunner I had my hands full right now. I haven't had a chance to talk to Zayden about the possible collaboration."

"How about this, come in and let me show you the operation. We could really use a guy like you on the occasional tricky ones. Besides, Kayla would be excited to see you again."

Damn, he'd be opening that can of worms again. He was in a better place now. It might work, or it might consign him to another long period of comparing everyone he dated to her.

"All right. I have the Foundation Gala event tonight and a meeting tomorrow morning, but I could pop over after lunch. Give me your address."

"We have tickets for that event, so we'll see you tonight, but I don't imagine any real business can get accomplished there."

"No, schmoozing for funds is the real reason for tonight. I can shoot for 1pm tomorrow if that works."

"Come for lunch. Kayla doesn't teach tomorrow, and she makes us a meal if she has the time. I'll give her a call. Otherwise, it's cold cuts and chips or takeout. Here's the address."

RIVER LOOKED UP FROM an introduction and saw her across the crowded ballroom floor. It was the annual benefit for the foundation. He hadn't even contemplated a woman to warm his bed in months, but the sight of Ms. Rhea changed all that. He'd recently tried to date, but he couldn't stop thinking of Kayla. Her vulnerability, her humor, her passion all came rushing at him, and that was the end of the date. After leaving Kayla with her father on the tarmac in Seattle over a year ago, his life had grown hectic. Hell, he was in an almost survival mode on some days, glad to live to fight another day in the business world. He understood what others meant when they described the boardroom as a jungle.

Every time he saw Kayla's picture or read her name, his cock did a jig. He stalked her on all media. He needed to purge her from his system. He needed to possess her. He was a realist, and, without either claiming or purging, he would be useless to move on. He'd proven that.

He was in the middle of planning the Foundation's annual project. This benefit would raise more funds for the project, and later, they would go dig wells, right after he dealt with the Kayla issue. He caught her eye from across the room, his cock stood at attention, and his mind quickly began to strategize how he would proceed. His military expertise stood him in good stead once again. Since resigning his commission, he found that his head for strategizing quick on the ground and logical thought processing was not as common as he thought it might be. His dad had lined things out to him not too long ago when River complained about the lack of common sense in the world.

"Don't be fooled. Common sense is not common, especially these days. No one takes the time to savor, to think about things, it's all impulse and reaction." He couldn't have been more right.

River continued to stare across the room, hesitant to break the connection with those eyes he had decided were the color of the Aegean Sea and that intelligent face primed for action. Kayla turned away, ending the contact. For now. River concentrated on stilling his pulse as he approached her, slipping seamlessly into her cocktail group, entering the conversation quietly. Kayla watched him closely before smiling warmly. Her eyes dilated, and her chest heaved. She felt it too. He had her; she was his. Others had looked longingly at him, but this one, this one he wanted.

As the group was chatting, a server came in behind Kayla, bumping into her, jostling her and the tray the server held. Kayla stepped back into River, who automatically put his hand against the small of her back. Wrapping the other arm around the front of her hip, he glided her out of harm's way. Her delicate scent, light and fresh, wafted up, intermingling with his next breath. Euphoria.

His fingers tingled as he held them against the small of her back, electrifying him. The air fairly crackled with the energy between them.

He caught her look of surprise that quickly returned to heat when her eyes connected with his. The attraction unmistakable, River needed to put his tactic into full play. His cock jumped for joy in anticipation of finally finding relief after his long-suffering dry spell.

Their stare became intense, nearly eliciting a groan from River when Kayla put her tongue out to skim her bottom lip before pressing her teeth into the flesh. He wanted to lick that lip, bite it, suck it, and lavish it with attention. His desire for her ramped exponentially. Only years of training on how to maintain silence stopped River's verbal appreciation of her beauty. He wanted her for as long as he could have her, and her answering look responded with the same desire. His cock, however, felt no urge to comply with orders to stand down.

The spell shattered when she stepped out of his hold and thanked him. She put out her hand, and, as her fingers curled around to clasp his own, she put her other hand on top of his. The move said she wanted to cement the link. Excellent, because that was his plan.

"Thank you, Mr. Bennett, for saving me again. It is becoming a habit."

"Good habits should be nurtured, don't you think, Miss Rhea? I have been following your work." Her face showed a flicker of surprise, a pink of embarrassment.

"Thank you for the save, Mr. Bennett." The reference to their first meetings obvious to them alone.

"River."

"It's a lovely gathering this evening, River."

"Yes, that was the intent. I can take no credit. Even my MC comments were predominately another's work."

"Yes, but your responsibilities are tremendous."

He nodded. "They can be, but the military trained me well in the art of delegation, and tonight, you see before you one of those excellent outcomes."

"Ah, something I am not well versed in, delegation, but I can appreciate the advantages of learning."

"I've seen your name on articles about your adventures."

"Really? I guess I never thought you were even aware of what I write or at least not interested in."

"Everything you do interests me. I remember our brief time fondly and often."

"I remember you too, fondly. And often."

River saw her adorable blush. She was embarrassed and, if he was reading her right, as aroused as he. River would need to seek out the men's room soon, just to take the edge off, if things didn't calm down so he could finish the evening. He noticed she was antsy as well.

"If you will excuse me, River..."

"Of course, except... may I take you into dinner at seven?"

She nodded hesitantly in his direction, carefully avoiding his eyes. "Didn't you come with your own date to escort?"

Once he knew she would be coming tonight, no thought about a date ever crossed his mind. He glanced around at the still chatting and yet oh so watchful group around them. "No, because once I heard you were coming, I didn't want one. But, of course, you might have brought one... probably brought one."

She shook her head. "No. Thank you for the offer. I would be delighted."

Whew, iceberg avoided. "At just before seven, I'll need to be at the podium to announce dinner. Will you wait for me there?"

"Yes, see you then."

She nodded to those also standing around them and left. River noticed her voice was tremoring slightly, her skin giving off the sweet scent of heated emotion. He watched her wipe her hands on her skirt, and then her arms wrapped her waist. All signs of turmoil. Good, he wanted to make her sweat. She had that same effect on him.

Soon after Kayla left his company to walk towards the bathroom, River's assistant told him he needed to move toward the podium to give the first of his short spiels to their gathered guests. It was time to be the master of ceremony and start collecting those donations.

What he would've rather done at that moment didn't include talking. He wanted to follow Kayla and run his hand through her perfectly coiffured hair. He would release all the pins that forced the wild tresses into compliance. He yearned to weave his hands through the free-falling silken locks. He could almost imagine his fingers closing around their thick strands, immobilizing her head as he lowered his lips to savor hers.

He wanted to taste her sweetness and push his tongue into the erotic velvety moistness of her mouth, savoring what he was sure would be ambrosia. He yearned to remove her clothing one piece at a time, slowly enjoying the unveiling of her perfect skin and voluptuous body. She had already given him a hint of her treasures tonight, with her overflowing bust line peeking out of her bodice.

Her sensual curvy hips swayed as she walked, and River knew her legs to be as long as her flowing skirt. River remembered long smooth thighs that flowed onto delicate ankles now strapped into those rather high heels of hers. He'd only ever seen her legs battered and bruised. He longed to see them unblemished.

After first engaging the crowd, River looked for his reward. He saw her dancing with a high-ranking Naval official and decided he would not interfere. It would be difficult to keep to his decision, though. That woman would be the death of him, now that he'd decided to claim her. Damn the age difference. He maintained his strength and virility and was still in the prime of his life. He could keep up with her and her impulsivity for decades.

For the rest of this evening, except for dinner, he would need to play host to the well-populated room, and for that, he was thankful. His ambitious projects demanded he encourage larger donations to continue their work at the level they currently operated. He would do a smaller project next year, but this year it needed to be impressive. He might get some additional funds to throw at Kayla's work, as they had previously discussed. That is if she accepted it.

KAYLA RUSHED INTO THE posh ladies' room outside the hotel's ballroom entrance, sinking into the comfy sofa while regaining her composure. She'd had to practically rush from the presence of the man who filled so many of her dreams, otherwise, she would have thrown herself at River Bennett. It wouldn't seem very dignified, but in all honesty, if she stayed next to him, she would have given him all kinds of truth. Her dreams about this man still made her blush.

River was way out of her league. She'd had no idea until she saw him from across the room how much he could affect her. Earlier in the evening, she immediately honed in on those penetrating, assessing dark eyes as his glance swept the room. His smile was unmistakable.

He'd saved her life. No doubt, it influenced her thoughts towards him. Tonight, though, had Kayla never met him before, she'd have noticed the way he carried himself confidently, exuding wealth, position, and power. His bulky biceps and muscular thighs that made his slacks cry for mercy had her begging for the same. His strength had thrilled her then and now. Yet, this time, he had a relaxed feel about him that put her at ease.

She'd watched him work the room for a few moments before their eyes met. Even with their distance apart, she could see his eyes gentle and heat with interest, possibly desire before turning to respond to another guest. Regardless of who they were as people in this world, she was inexplicably drawn to River. She almost didn't come tonight, but her brothers urged her to, and now she wondered if they knew she had been flying a holding pattern waiting for River.

Kayla stood up abruptly from the powder room sofa, determined to find out more about him. He had the perfect name for someone who quietly appeared at her side and, with great ease, slid into the ongoing conversation. She wished she could boast that kind of confidence in these types of high society events. She knew she sported a reputation for not playing the game as other women did. She wasn't a socialite. Nor was she striving to break the glass ceiling in commerce. Nothing put Kayla off more than pretentiousness or aggression. She would not embody those traits to spread her message.

Maybe after spending some time with River, learning about him, she would be able to purge him from her system and drop out of the holding pattern. Kayla had never been a stupid woman. If she didn't figure this out with him now, she would be obsessed. She already had one all-consuming interest. How would she ever deal with another? No, another passion would never fit in her world. Would it?

She looked around to see if her father or one of her brothers were near. Kayla looked for Robbie but held a sneaking suspicion that her eldest brother had gone to find a place to ride out the event. These types of gatherings normally irritated him. He did it for the business and for their father, but he tried never to stay long. So why did he work so hard to get her here?

By five minutes to seven, the room echoed with conversation. Sarge expressed his surprise that River asked her to go into dinner with him by raising his eyebrow and gracing her with one of his long, contemplative stares before he spoke.

"To my knowledge, River has no wives, no children, and no present girlfriends."

"Good, no one will be angry if I sit with him at dinner, then."

"I wouldn't say that, but he appears to be his own man. If he asked you, he meant it. If the two of you want to sit at dinner together, you should. It's just..."

"What? It's just what?"

"I'm worried that you're stuck on this *thing*. That both of you are perseverating over each other because of what happened to bring you two together in the first place. It was traumatic, and the memories are tainted, inaccurate."

"You mean the abduction? You think my memories are making him into something he isn't, and he has the same problem?"

"Right. I think you both are harboring an unnatural connection because he rescued

you."

"Do you think he isn't good enough or has some issue I should know about?"

"Nope. He's a stand-up guy and has no issues that I know of, but you're my daughter,

and I don't want you hurt and if I'm right—"

"Okay. I'll do the best I can to not fall into a deep dark hole if we don't click at dinner. Dad, I'm more intelligent than that."

"I hope so because I would hate to have to send in one of the team to straighten him out."

"It might take two." Kayla grinned at the brooding look her father gave her before she kissed his cheek. "Don't worry so much."

"It's my job as your dad."

Now here she stood, feeling awkward, and yet her belly was jumpy, primed to see River. She was scouring the room for his lean, muscular body when hot breath bathed her left ear and cheek, sending delicious shivers through her.

"Looking for me?"

Her eyes jerked up, landing on River. When she saw his face, she couldn't stop her smile. "Hi. Looking for me?"

"Or someone remarkably similar to you."

"Hi beautiful, you're like the summer sun, bright, warm, and mine to enjoy."

"Mmm, thank you? I don't think anyone has ever called me sunshine before."

"They were all blind. You are enticing in your glow."

"It might be you that draws that out of me. Or maybe you've had a touch too much cocktail." She arched her brow

"Brat. It's your presence. I'll do my best to keep the look of happiness on your face. Let me announce dinner, and then we will go in. Come stand next to me."

"Oh, I couldn't," she protested as he swept her along with him.

Holding her hand, River spoke into the microphone. "It's time to gather your partner and go into dinner. I found mine."

He squeezed her hand, and Kayla saw camera flashes. As they made their way to their places, she admonished him.

"Silly man, now people will make all sorts of speculations about you."

He laughed. "Oh? Why, are you beyond gossip?"

"No, because I'm not important here, or gorgeous but you—"

River's look turned serious as he spoke for her ears only. "Stop right there. In my world, ladies get hot seats when they denigrate themselves *before* they get hot sex."

Her words faltered. "N-not at all, honest assessment is not denigration, it is realism. I don't feel bad if it's an unavoidable truth."

"Then, you're blind. I'll work on that."

She chuckled. "Thank you."

Dinner was a bit more taxing than Kayla had expected, but as the last course ended, River reached over and kissed her hand, then her cheek. More camera flashes were accompanied by more murmurings.

Kayla looked reproachfully at him. "River."

"Shh, we can tease them, can't we? Besides, who knows, they may be getting an exclusive?"

"An exclusive to what?"

"Our first dinner."

"Oh. Well, it is our first dinner."

"Our first date, the start of it all." The intensity of his look told her of his seriousness. Her body flushed in a heated response. River turned to respond to another guest, and the moment was gone.

The long night was almost over. River steadfastly kept Kayla by his side the rest of the evening, catering to her needs, including finding her a seat to rest her feet when she whispered she wanted to take her shoes off.

"So do it."

"What? No, I couldn't."

He shrugged and had a chair brought over for her to sit on. "Sorry, baby, just one more hour," he promised.

"I'm fine."

She grimaced as her voice sounded tortured even to her own ears. She sat, and the relief was almost orgasmic. Almost. She would not let aching feet stop her from sharing a bed with River if the opportunity arose. She'd come this far once before, but this time there would be no emergency to call him away. Kayla was either going to rid her system of her yearnings or, much more likely, she'd want to stake her claim to his bed, his body, his mind and his soul. Who was this daring woman? Kayla kinda liked her.

River stood behind her chair and rubbed her neck with his thumb. So familiar. So hot. Kayla was almost glad for the distraction her dad and brothers offered when they came to collect her and say their good-nights.

"River, man, this was something, but once a year is all my blood can take. I might've made some connections of my own. Thanks for the invite. Kayla, you ready?"

"Oh, um, I-I well—"

"I'll get her home."

Her father looked at River rather intensely for a moment. "Tonight?"

"Dad, stop, I'm a—"

"I hope not, sir."

Robbie and Taren sported *the look*, the one that said they were going to fight for her honor just as they did when she was little.

Kayla looked up at River and stood. "River..."

She should say something more, protest stronger, but the predatory look in his eyes made her belly drop to the floor. She could feel the heat rising in her cheeks, the tingling reignited in her core, and her pussy become slippery. Kayla closed her mouth. This man affected her like no other, and she didn't want to change his mind. River smiled and nodded.

Her father stood for another moment, not saying more before he kissed her cheek and left. Her brothers gave River a protective stare and communicated the only way guys did with nods, and grunts, then they also kissed her cheek and left. It was as though they were marking her for protection. She smiled. Men.

Chapter Seven

River had not been celibate since leaving the Army, but he also didn't offer any return encounters after one night. No woman came to his bed, nor did he stay the night. He slept alone in his own place. Women tended to get clingy with more than one night. Ever since he'd met this woman, he was hooked. He'd held her on the transport home, watching as she finger-combed her bedraggled hair and ripped the hem off her tee-shirt to tie it up. This girl was practical and still beautiful beneath all that dirt and fear. He'd given up a long time ago trying to erase her from his memory. An image of her flashed through his mind every time he saw another woman with her general description.

Now that he had her, he wouldn't let her go until she was out of his system. River, being a realist, recognized he might never purge her. Kayla looked up at him after he shook her youngest brother's hand. River understood he was asking a lot from her father when he laid his cards on the table. He wanted to take Sarge's daughter home with him, and he didn't guarantee that he was bringing her back.

River was taking a risk because, as any man or beast knows, you don't crap in your own yard. That was just what River was doing, or at least his actions could have the same result if he didn't tread carefully. He might have entertained working with Sarge occasionally, and the wrong move with this woman would end that chance. Still, regardless of the fallout, Kayla would be coming home with him tonight and staying for as long as they agreed. She wanted it, and he wanted it. They were consenting adults, and he planned on taking full advantage of that fact.

River leaned down and whispered to Kayla. "Sorry, I just have a few more people to send off, then we'll be out the door. Normally I would be able to leave but," he shrugged, "I'm the host. Are you okay to wait?"

"Of course, I am. I'm not such a child that I must be entertained to keep from becoming bored or naughty." Her voice sounded petulant. "Sorry. That didn't come out the way I intended. I'm fine. I can wait."

"I hope I can," he murmured.

River shook hands with another dozen or so men accompanied by lovely women who were quite obviously not all spouses. In fact, some looked young enough to be their daughters but sported no familial likenesses. When the last May to December couple walked past them, and the last woman in the room finished making a pass at River, he stretched out his hand.

"And now it's time to retrieve your wrap because your chariot awaits, my dear."

"You are too kind, sir. Please lead the way." The tired look disappeared in the sparkle of her eyes.

River's grip tightened, and his lips brushed her cheek. "I'm going to hold you to that later." He felt her slight tremor, and it pleased him.

River preferred to drive himself on nights like this. When many others were being chauffeured, he declined the offer. His father, however, enjoyed it, allowing him to concentrate on other things during the ride. River could see the benefit of that, so sometimes he indulged himself, but not tonight, not with Kayla. He wanted her all to himself.

River lived in a large apartment building that the corporation leased. He was on the ninth floor and shared it with his sister and husband when they were in town. His parents were on the top. River's parents lived there when in Seattle and the rest of the time in Alaska, as did he. Being close at hand sometimes made things more convenient. He smiled when Kayla oohed and aahed the hallway artwork and the entryway to his apartment that allowed one to see out over the city from the doorway.

"River, this is gorgeous. I'm not much for living in the city, but this could change a person's mind."

"I agree. There have to be trade-offs when staying in the city, and this is some enticing trade-off. Would you like a glass of wine?"

"I better not. I've probably drunk enough as it is."

River's voice was firmer this time. "How much did you drink this evening? Are you feeling the effects of it?"

"Don't worry. Yes, I indulged more than I normally do, but that was at the beginning of the night, so any of its euphoric effects have long dissipated."

"Let me see if I can't recapture that feeling for you."

Leaning in, he captured her lips with his as he drew her shawl from her. His hands slid across her shoulders and up into her hair, anchoring her head as he deepened the kiss. He allowed his lips to slide down her throat, kissing the pulse beating rapidly at the base of her neck. He continued kissing, nipping at her exposed skin, then letting his tongue soothe the spot to comfort her.

Her breath came more rapidly, and her skin tasted of the sweet and salty flavor of perspiration as it dampened everywhere his lips teased. He loved her little whimpers, her murmurings as his hands sought the firm nipples beneath her dress. He allowed himself an answering strangled sound before he took her lips again in a harder kiss, possessing what he wanted. She gave all that he asked and offered more. He released her lips and moved back just a few inches. He felt his cock jerk painfully when she reached out her tongue and traced his lips.

"You're a little minx, and I hope you know how to play with this raging fire you're stoking."

She whispered her response. "I'm sure I can handle it."

With an unsettled moan, River leaned down and shoved his tongue into her mouth, seeking hers. They tangled almost frantically as he swung her up into his arms and strode to his bedroom. He leaned over his bed hurriedly as he reached into the side table drawer and pulled out a handful of wrappers that crinkled.

"Is all that for me?" Kayla asked seductively.

"No, they are for me. *I* am for you. Be a good girl and take your clothes off. I could take them off, but I'm not so sure I can be as careful with them as you need me to be. That's assuming, of course, you're going to wear them again, because if you don't, then I can take them off."

"This dress was rather expensive. I better remove it myself."

Kelli leaned up to undress, unbuttoning the top and wiggling until she was free. She reached up to unhook her bra, and his hands were on top of hers.

"Let me," he said as he unhooked her, tossing the material to the floor.

He returned to massage her ample breasts and loving her ever-hardening nipples that gave away her excitement. His hand slid down her sides and crooked his thumbs, sliding them under the elastic of her panties at either hip, slowly drawing them down her thighs. He leaned in and kissed her belly, running his tongue over her neatly trimmed entrance pointing the way to the guardian outer lips of her pussy.

Kayla's hands began a frantic search for his buttons, making several desperate sounds when she was not immediately successful in releasing him from his bonds.

"Shh, I can get it. Let go, baby."

"I wanted to undress you."

"Next time, I'll do it this time."

When she didn't slow her attempts, River moved away and strengthened his tone. "No, I said I would do it. You can next time. Stop, baby."

Her hands fell, and her wiggling slowed as she dropped to a sitting position on the bed. He didn't want her libido to cool, so he didn't take his eyes from her and began bumping her legs wide with his thighs as he took the vest off. Several buttons popped on his shirt in his attempt to speed the process. Her eyes widened.

"Scoot up on the bed and open those gorgeous legs of yours. Give me room to visit."

She nodded and moved into the center of the bed. Her thighs spread slightly. River kicked off his pants and underwear, yanking the socks off to land on top of his clothing pile.

"Now, sweetheart, that isn't going to be nearly enough." He swatted her inner thigh and moved to repeat the process on her other one. She whimpered but didn't widen.

He grinned. "Have it your way. I like to be the one running the show in most areas. I can give the reins over occasionally in my daily life, but rarely in the bedroom. So one last chance, before I teach you what disobedience will get you."

He tapped her inner thighs harder.

KAYLA LOVED THE PLAY. The little taps were stingy but not un-comfortable. She loved the way it made her pink bits twitch and her breasts tingle. She watched him roll her over and readied herself for the swats he laid on her right cheek. Her juices flowed.

"Mmm, do it again." She looked over at him.

River raised his right eyebrow and hummed. "My baby likes a little slap and tickle, huh?"

"Please," she begged.

He rolled her to slap the other cheek. "Now open so I can see how wet you are for me." This time she spread them wide. The heat from those few smacks made her warm all over. She'd always known she was intrigued by spanking, but no one had ever spanked her before. She'd been a good kid, but she could learn how to be naughty in the bedroom if she could get these types of results. Kayla lifted her pelvis to help him find her treasures and yelped at the slap on her pussy. She grunted her surprise.

"I'm the boss here, Kayla. I'll decide what you need. And I think what you need now is me."

Kayla watched as River took one hardened nipple into his mouth and sucked with ever-increasing strength as he made her writhe with flames of passion. He loved the other breast equally before kissing down her belly. Kayla felt him nip at her labia before peeling back her lower lips to expose her slippery center. She felt herself panic. Her very experienced girlfriend in college once told her, *Men don't really like to taste women, Kayla, didn't anyone ever tell you before?*"

"Don't... I mean, I don't expect you to."

He stopped, poised above her most intimate area. "Good to know, but are you saying you don't like it, or you don't think I'll like it?"

"I don't know if I'll like it because..." she shrugged her shoulders slightly, "well, I know guys don't enjoy it."

"Sweetheart, I don't know who told you that, but it's a lie. Men love it. This man loves it."

"Oh." He resumed his task. "Mmm, that feels so nice."

"That's what I like to hear," he murmured. "Hold still while I enjoy my second dessert."

Shock waves of pleasure rolled over her as he licked and nibbled, sucking on her sensitive clit. She couldn't keep still any longer. The waves of sensation took her out to sea, tossing her like a rag doll then shooting her quickly to heaven.

"Again."

Kayla still felt the effects of the second orgasm when he pulled her legs over his shoulders and slid inside her. Kayla couldn't remember exactly the last time she slept with anyone, but it had been over a year, and the sheer bulk of River took her a few moments to adjust.

He was all business now, moving his cock to just the right angle as he pistoned in and out of her wet channel. Kayla could feel the familiar tingle of her clit as his thumb abraded it, sharing the slickness from her opening. The rhythmic in and out movement of River pounding her vagina brought on another overwhelming wave of euphoria. Kayla was losing control, waiting, urging the next cresting. The juices of arousal rolled down the valley between her cheeks to her bottom entrance, where it pooled. Another upsurge of heat rushed over her, lifting her up. River placed a finger at her anus and pressed inward.

She couldn't help the groan. She thought she would love anal play, but only once had anyone ever attempted it. It had proven to be greatly unsatisfying. Kayla thought it could be incredible with the right person. River pressed harder against the outer ring of muscle while slowing his cock's pace. It was as though he instinctively knew she wanted that bottom play as if he read her mind.

He pushed steadily, and the muscle burn scorched her. She whimpered, and he stopped for just a few seconds before moving in and out, his finger taking her bottom. The sensation was incredible.

"My baby likes that too? Good girl."

The rush of heat almost engulfed her at his praise. It gave her courage, and she opened her mouth to ask for more, but he was way ahead of her, adding more pressure with his big thick finger. His hands were not hardened, but they were not soft either. It was a good combination of rough and smooth.

"I'm close," she rasped.

"No, you hold on. We go together this time. Do you hear me? Hold on, or I will punish your greediness."

"What? I can't hold back."

"You had better learn fast. You'll enjoy it more if you do."

Because she couldn't come, the urgency to reach completion was nearly overwhelming. "River, I promise, I'll learn, but I can't stop now. I want to please you, but I have to come." Her mournful wail rose as she gave in to her desperate, all-consuming need to fall over the cliff of eroticism.

The next sensation, followed by any meaningful thought, was River's pounding into Kayla and an almost immediate loud grunting sigh. Fast and then slow. Suddenly, hands massaged her breasts gently before she dipped her head to her pillow, and River rolled off her body. He tied and disposed of the condom, making a muted thud as he threw it in some container beside the bed.

He reached and pulled her onto his chest and kissed her lips. "You're hot when you're naughty, baby. There is so much more that we will explore. I never thought about how adventuresome you would be, and it surprises me that you'd be so brave this soon in our relationship. I love it."

"Why, thank you. I think." She snuggled on his chest and tweaked his nipple, licking the one next to her mouth. He hissed. "Relationship?"

"Yes, relationship, because I'm not letting you go unless I'm sure we don't both want this permanently. Right now, it sounds damn good to me. But I also said hot and naughty, did you hear me?"

"But naughty in a good way."

"Naughty as in disobeyed, naughty."

"Oh." Kayla tried to remember what rule she had broken. "But I honestly couldn't hold back. It's mean to ask me to wait."

"So we will need to practice until you gain more control, much more control. But, for now, it's punishment." She watched his arm move, and his hand came down on her ass hard.

She screeched. "Ow. That isn't the feel-good kind of smacks. That hurt, River."

"Nope." The other hand landed on her other cheek. "It's punishment for coming without permission."

"I said I couldn't stop. I never tried to stop before."

She wiggled her bottom because the heat from just those two swats did funny things to her insides and then began morphing into what she now knew she loved.

He kissed her lips and said, "Two more."

He landed two more stinging swats and then spread her legs wide with his knees as he kneeled between them. Sliding his hand between her thighs, he maneuvered down to her clit, which he rubbed. She jumped with the suddenness of the assault.

"Oh, I'm feeling my control leaving already." She tried hard to stem her ragged breathing with little luck.

"Up and up and stop."

It was a strange feeling to almost crest and then have the sensation taken away. "River. That isn't nice. It's cruel."

"I'm helping you learn, and I like it when you're so close to the edge. You take on this euphoric expression, then when I stop, you look almost wounded. You're adorable when you don't get your treat."

"But why do I need to learn to stop from orgasming? I love orgasms."

"You'll love them more if you learn to delay your gratification. The fireworks are even better. And because I asked you."

"Oh, fine. But then you should have to stop and hold out too."

"Baby, I wanted to shoot my wad the second I saw your body. I think possibly before that. I've been hard just hoping to get a glimpse of you tonight. Control I have and control you're going to get. Let's start again."

Chapter Eight

The next day at quarter to noon, found River anticipating meeting up with Kayla Rhea again. He remembered her this morning as he left for the office. Her heavy curtain of golden amber hair fanned out over the pillow, her soft snore calling him to take her again before he left, but he wouldn't. He knew some women were embarrassed or felt out of place the morning after sex, even out of this world sex, so he left her with a note on the bathroom mirror.

Would she be happy to see him today, or was last night more than enough for her? He knew they had wanted to hook up several years ago, but fate intervened then, as well. She was much too young for him, and he was too preoccupied for her. Then, that recovery in Somalia had been another opportunity that he hadn't acted on soon enough.

He felt like a lot of life had happened since she'd initiated that goodbye kiss, which topped the charts of his most memorable good-byes ever. They hadn't even talked last night. Hadn't discussed what she'd been doing the last year or so. She didn't say, but he had a feeling she'd been thinking of him.

After last night, he didn't have to worry if the memories of an event she would rather forget would stop her from being receptive to him. If she was as engaging today as she was last night, he would ask her out. If not, he'd better move on and start dating more because he had to either bring her into his world or obliterate that meeting out of his mind.

River pushed the doorbell to Robert Rhea's home. The house was large, well maintained. He loved his secluded place in Port Refuge, but Seattle had some nice homes, and this was one. Not in a flashy neighborhood but one that it was obvious the owners were proud of their places. The door opened, and he looked up into the sparkling eyes of Kayla Rhea. Yep, they were still on. Their night of sex was obviously amazing to not only him. Now, how the hell did he untie his tongue?

KAYLA GRINNED AS SHE looked at his handsomely stern face. His answering smile demolished the stiffness from his posture, and he relaxed. For a reason she couldn't have explained, she flung herself into his arms, never thinking it might take him off guard, and they would both end up on the front porch looking up. That didn't happen, though. He caught her and dipped his head to take her lips with his. The zing from that connection ignited her to a quiver. Suddenly she wanted inside him, in his very skin. This tidal wave of emotion couldn't be normal, right?

The kiss seemed to go on forever until there was a loud clearing of a male throat behind them. The lip massage ended as abruptly as it had begun. Taking a quick glance into River's eyes, she saw he had softened. His brown eyes were warm and indulgent, his cock showed interest too. She gave him a sheepish grin and turned around.

"Hello, Sir," said River as he nodded in Sarge's direction.

As he reached out to shake her father's hand, River snaked the other around her waist. She should be more embarrassed than she was, but the tingle of excitement that raced up her back told her that was not going to happen. Sarge raised an eyebrow but kept his own counsel as they entered the foyer.

"River, good to see you again. You may be spending time with my daughter, but you can still call me Sarge."

River nodded.

"How about we let Kayla finish lunch while we sit in the living room and discuss what this might look like."

"Dad, I already know what you do."

"Good, so you aren't missing out on anything. I'm starved, honey."

"You ate breakfast."

"Yes, I did, and now it's lunch. Please?"

Her harrumph was louder than she had expected. River squeezed her hip, where his hand still sat. She felt chastised and bouncy all at the same time. She didn't want to hear about the company, she wanted to stay with River. Her father was likely going to interrogate River on his behavior with his daughter.

"What was that you said, dear?" asked her father in an innocent voice that she knew was a cover-up for either humor or a challenge.

River's hand slid over slightly to sit at the camber of her bottom. Then the man had the audacity to pat her in a warning. She was surrounded by macho men, and this one she had invited to be familiar with her. She needed her head examined, but her pink bits disagreed. Today, they won.

"Fine, we should eat in fifteen minutes. Can you cram all the parts you don't want me to hear in that time, dad?"

Sarge chuckled. "I should be able to get the worst of it over with by then. Thanks, hon."

True to her word, they were sitting down to eat in fifteen minutes, but she served them at the kitchen table. As usual, men never noticed. River gave her a searching look but didn't try to commandeer her as he had after her bold move at the door. He did sit next to her though, his warm hand settled on her thigh, causing her belly to riot. She tried to ignore the urge to crawl in his lap. Just at that moment, he let his hand slide down to possess the inner part of her thigh and rubbed. She gushed and blushed. And gritted her teeth.

Rob, always the geek, sat down and stared at River. He reached over, nodded as he shook his hand, then simply sat; not eating, not joining in the conversation, just stared. Robbie stared at Kayla next before returning his gaze to River. Then he nodded, filled his plate, and joined in as though he decided it was safe to do so. None of the men seemed disturbed about his behavior. What was that, a guy code for something? She hated men sometimes. Just as she was going to comment, Rob spoke.

Looking at her father, he asked, "So, did you finally find a way to get the one man you've been looking for to fill the slot?"

"What slot?" asked Kayla.

Taren walked into the kitchen. "Sorry I'm late," he said as he leaned down and kissed Kayla's head. He hesitated for a brief moment and then put his hand out to River as he sat on the other side of him and filled his plate. "This is worth the extra PT.," he said as he filled his plate with chicken and dumplings. Her family was acting off. Kayla felt certain that none of what was going on right now would have happened if River weren't there. But why?

She tried to bring things into some kind of natural order. "What slot were you looking to fill, dad?"

"Oh, right. Well, River here is a strategist. I can sit in the Com Center and give out orders, but on long runs, I really need someone who has a talent for making things work like they should. Draw us the map to go by, the play by play. I'm trying to persuade him to join us on the more challenging assignments. You know, the ones that will take a light but decisive hand. We don't have many, but we do have them."

"You know, that actually makes sense," said Kayla.

Sarge feigned hurt feelings, but her brothers laughed, and River smiled. Good, now maybe they could get back to normal. Except the wrong normal, evidently.

"What's your impression of the African coast these days, River?" asked Sarge.

"Well, sir—"

"Dad, that isn't fair. I said I'd wait until summer, so trying to get support for your archaic reasoning is just low, even for you." Her face heated.

"It was a normal question, Kayla. You can be so defensive, honey." Sarge acted innocent, but Kayla knew that he was conniving.

"Uh-huh. Looks like this is your last home-cooked meal for a while."

"Honey, don't be that way. We talk about all sorts of places." The men discussed the recent intel coming out of the region. Kayla did hear the concern in their voices and the intensity when recalling certain events. Just when she thought they had forgotten her, River squeezed her thigh. They had circled back to why Kayla should not go back to Africa.

"That is another reason why she shouldn't go back. Women, especially blondes, are magnets for kidnappers," said Taren.

"You do know that last trip of Kayla's was a setup," said River. "I'd be worried it would happen again when others set it up."

"I agree, but I've had a helluva time figuring out where it went sour," said Rob.

River nodded and turned to Kayla. "What does the organization say?"

She smiled warmly at River's introduction of her inability to have stopped the happenings that day. "Nothing. They said it was tragic, but they had no prior knowledge about the events before they occurred."

"That was the official statement?" asked River.

Kayla sighed. "In writing."

River took a bite of the apple pie she sat in front of him. "Mmm, delicious. Okay, if that was the response, then we have some things to work out." He took another bite and checked his watch before feeding the last bit to Kayla. "Unfortunately, I can't do that right now. I have a meeting in about thirty minutes. My assistant is going to have my scalp if I don't get there in time." He turned to Kayla. "Excellent lunch. Best I've had in weeks."

She grinned. "Liar."

River shook his head. "No, really. I usually get whatever someone grabs for me. Hold on." Pulling out his phone, he said, "I'll check to make sure I'm not double booking, but would you be available for dinner with me?"

"Um, sure." She took a quick glance around to see her father sporting his pensive face, Taren was obviously surprised, and Robbie was clicking away on his iPad. She imagined something they said had him researching.

"Great. I'm free after this meeting, so how about seven?"

"Good, but I'll be at my studio. I have a project I'm working on, and I get more done if I'm there."

River looked around the table. "I get it, less testosterone. Okay, give me your number." He sent her a text, and the phone on the counter dinged. "Now, when you get a chance, send me your address." River pushed back from the table. "Sorry, I have to eat and run, but I'll consider your offer and see what I can do, Sarge."

"Great." The men stood and shook hands in the kitchen, and Kayla walked him out to his car.

"Thank you for the offer, but you don't have to take me out."

"True, but I want to have dinner with you. Your family is great, but I want to spend time with you alone."

"I'd like that. And River, do you really think my trip was a setup?"

"Positive. I just don't know how or why. We can talk more later." He dropped a gently possessive kiss on her lips. "Send me that address."

"I will." She stood in the driveway until River was out of sight.

Preparing to go to her studio, Kayla stood in front of her closet and began to worry she had nothing to wear. Somewhere in the far reaches of her mind, she heard her mother say, "A little black dress is classy and shows any jewelry off well. Don't forget when you get older and someone wants to take you out, a little black dress will impress them every time." Her mother had smiled and kissed her cheek before donning her own dress and going out to dinner.

Snatching the needed clothing, she raced to her studio apartment, determined to get some real work done. After doing a quick tidying up, she pulled out her computer, set the alarm, and began to work on the next article, complete with photo commentary.

At six, the alarm went off. Kayla was reluctant to stop, but she needed time to shower and do a little primping, so she found a stopping point, closed her computer, and walked into the shower.

At two minutes to seven, there was a knock at Kayla's door. She checked through the glass and opened the door. A huge smile on her face met his pleasantly surprised look. She suddenly felt shy.

"You look amazing."

"Hi. Come in, and thank you. I hope it's alright. I thought I'd go simple in case you take me to a more comfortable, less dressy place. I wore pearls if it wasn't that informal. I can change the jewelry if it's too much."

"Stop talking. You're stunning. Besides, I'd take you with a potato sack."

"Darn, I threw my last one out." Kayla bent to pick up her shawl for the cooler evening air. "Oh," she said as a playful swat landed on her butt. "Hey," her hand covered the targeted spot and looked up questioningly.

"You earned it. I could get used to this."

"Ha! You and every other male in my world these days. Feel better now?"

He shrugged. "A little. Want me to make it feel better?" God, she did with every fiber of her being. Too soon, too soon. "Maybe later? I'm starving. Where are you taking me? Somewhere good, I hope. With normal-sized portions."

"As a matter of fact, I am. Or I was. You're in a mouthy mood. I might change my mind." He said with mock indecision.

Kayla giggled. "Okay, I give up. I'm sorry. Will you please take me to this yummy place for dinner because I am about to eat my own arm?"

"I've heard that isn't as appetizing as one might first think." He helped her settle her shawl around her shoulders.

"Now, whose being a smart ass?"

"You are mouthy. Swearing doesn't sound good on a woman."

The look she tried to sport was an exaggerated version of disbelief?

"Um, you do know who my father and brothers are? You've met them. Swearing is part of the rite of passage around there."

"I don't like it. It's unladylike, and more than that, it demeans other's thoughts of a woman. Most people don't like too much swearing, and when a woman does it, it sounds forced and crude."

She sighed. "Still starving here, so I'll agree to put a lid on it as much as possible if you agree to get me fed soon."

"As you wish. And thank you. I know it's old fashioned but..." River shrugged.

Kayla tried not to think about how he had gotten his way even though she had first thought she was in control of the moment since most men would be trying to impress her. Evidently, not River's style, but he did impress her with his lack of hesitancy to lead the way. He propelled her down the hallway with his hand on her back after locking the door.

His palm slid down to the general area he'd swatted her butt, which tingled again, only this time, because of his light touch. She nearly lifted her bottom to meet his slowly circling hand. Kayla worried she had no defenses against this sharply dressed, hot as sin businessman soldier. She had enough bossiness in her life, but River. Well, rules were meant to be broken, right? And just having a good time wasn't violating any standards, if she were careful.

She saw the sleek black car he led her to, and not knowing cars, she tried to glimpse the model placard, but it was a bit dark in this area of the lot. He helped her settle in her seat.

"Are the lights normally this dark?"

"In this part of the property? Yes."

"And where do you park?"

"Under that light right there if I can. I've had enough lectures from the guys to know not to go into dark corners. Besides, I don't sleep here often. Usually, I'm at the house."

"Good girl."

A-a-a-n-nd her panties were steaming. No change in her purse. Damn. She'd never needed it, but she had carried one for the first few years in college. No one ever made her need to use them, but tonight might be different. River reached and buckled her seatbelt, unleashing another little trickle. She thought she might have gotten just a slight whiff of her arousal. Hopefully, River wasn't that observant.

He settled into his seat and buckled up. Without looking in her direction, he started the car and put it into gear. "Your perfume is particularly nice. What's it called?"

Ode de embarrassment, she thought. "Shimmering Sand. It's spicy."

"Mmm. Yes, it is. And I understand scents are different according to the wearer's chemistry. Yours must be perfect with that particular fragrance."

"Um, thank you?"

"Yes, it's a compliment. Don't you get many of those?"

"Not like that. Well, not really. Most of the guys I hang out with are either ex-military working for the company, my brother's friends, or young adjuncts."

"Kayla, honey, I'm not sure if you noticed, but you are still young and an adjunct."

She grinned. "True, and you are ex-military."

"I prefer 'former' to 'ex.'"

"Touchy. Anyway, the military guys are too impressed with themselves and the adjuncts, too busy trying to impress."

"No one excites you."

"Not so far. Well, there was a man who did, but twice duty called, and I never figured out if it was the new girl thing or real desire he felt."

"I'll see if we can change that." He patted her thigh and turned into a parking lot.

Not knowing what to say to that statement, Kayla looked out the window and found her, and her red face sitting in his black sporty car was at one of her favorite restaurants. Greek, Sicilian, and Italian food.

"Oh, I love this place. Thank you for bringing me here, but usually, you need to have a reservation."

"I do."

"A week or more in advance." She added dubiously.

"They make exceptions for me." River said enigmatically. "You must not be that hungry if you are chatting out here instead of heading for the door."

"Wrong. Lead the way, and I hope you brought your wallet."

River laughed. "I'll manage."

As he had said, there was a reservation and a happy hostess ready to take them to a nice table in the corner. Once they sat, a man in a suit she recognized as one of the owners came to the table with a bottle of wine.

"Antonio." The men shook hands.

"Ah, Guerriero, you can't stay away." Turning to Kayla, Antonio beamed and reached for her hand that he patted and held it for a few moments. "And who is this? Il tuo amante?"

Kayla blushed. She knew enough of the Latin-based languages to know he asked if she was River's lover. What he called River was a mystery, though.

"Vedremo."

We'll see? Kayla wasn't sure, but that's what it sounded like. The man turned to Kayla, who was still blushing hotly. She imagined her face was glowing.

"This is a good man. You are safe with him." Antonio looked at her intently. "I know you, no? You have been in my ristorante before, no?"

Kayla nodded. "Yes, with my family. Three big, noisy men."

The man grinned broadly again. "Yes, Guerreros, like our River. I remember. He patted her hand and returned it to the table. I will take care of you two. Let me bring you a little something for your hungry belly, no? Elena will be your waitress. She is coming just now."

The energetic man hurried off after speaking briefly to Elena.

The dinner was divine, as always. Kayla found River had a dry sense of humor hidden under his enigmatic exterior. She liked it.

"I'd have thought you'd be in your island retreat by now. You're out of the Army."

"Yes, I am, but there are other commitments now. The foundation offices are here. I needed to attend the Gala, but I go back this weekend."

"But how do you do that and live in, where is it, Port Refuge?"

"Cache Island, yes, outside of Port Refuge. Well, you know about the Corporation and Foundation attached to it. I also have a personal office in my home, where at least half of my business is conducted. I have two assistants. One here, one in Port Refuge. Besides, I can hop a plane to Seattle in the morning, get my work done, and be home that night, if necessary."

"Wow, a rather long commute, though, right?"

"If I flew commercial. It's easier going in the morning by the commercial, small airport and all on the island, and in the winter, coming home isn't that difficult, either. Now summer is trickier because of tourists, fishermen, park rangers, and so many others getting in the way. Still, I wouldn't miss Alaska in the summer because of the inconvenience. You have to come to see my property and the world of freedom it opens up."

"Uh, I watched some of those off the grid, no modern conveniences TV shows. No, thank you. I'm spoiled and proud of it."

"You'll be pleasantly surprised if that is your image of Alaska and Alaskans. That version is true in some cases, but the vast majority get both the wilderness and the conveniences. We are just happy with less fanfare. Come with me this weekend. I'll have you back by Monday afternoon."

"What? Mm, probably not a good idea."

"Why not?"

"Well, for one, I hardly know you."

"You know me well enough to trust me to keep you safe." He lowered his voice and leaned into her. "Enough to have gone to bed with me."

He had her there. "Well, I don't want you to entertain me. That would be asking too much."

"We will entertain each other. Say yes, or is the woman who flies halfway across the world to get to Africa to help regardless of the danger afraid to go?"

"What? Not regardless of the danger, I mean, I do go, but I... okay, fine. When and where do I meet you, and what do I bring?"

"Tomorrow afternoon. I'll send you an itinerary. Bring clothes for about fifteen degrees cooler."

After enjoying the meal, they split a slice of cherry cheesecake. "Now, tell me what you know about the society you do your work with; there has to be a clue there."

"The setup? Right, well, I don't feel comfortable talking about it here, in public."

"Okay. So, let's grab the check and go back to my condo. It's closer than your studio and much closer than your dad's."

She hesitated and wondered if the invitation included sex. She hoped so. She wasn't against being with River, but she wasn't sure if her slippery nether region should be her deciding factor. Kayla decided she'd wanted him for a long time. Fate had brought them together, intimately more than enough times to believe it was a sign. When she decided to say yes, she looked up and saw River watching her.

"You decide on yes or no?"

"That obvious?"

He shrugged. "I don't think you're a rash person, regardless of your death wish in going back to tempt fate over and over again in your annual trips."

"Those are not rash decisions," she hissed.

"No? Then here is your chance to prove it to me."

"I don't have to prove it to anyone. Look, I'm tired of battling this corner of my life. It'd be nice to just have someone understand."

"Just for the record, I might understand your motives, but it may not be enough for me to agree that you go back. And I won't ever agree to you going alone."

"Then it's a good thing you won't be part of my decision." The look he gave her was full of so many things, none of which she wanted to explore at that moment.

RIVER PULLED INTO THE parking garage and hopped out. When he rounded the front of the vehicle, he was surprised Kayla was still sitting in the car, waiting for him to open her door and help her out. It was so unlike his girl, he wondered if he should be on his guard.

"I like that you wait for me, and I don't have to tell you to allow me to assist, but I am a little surprised."

"I might have grown up most of my childhood without a mom, but my dad was pretty good about telling me what men expect if they are worth their salt."

"Thank you."

She rolled her eyes, and River loved it. He placed his hand at the back of her neck and settled it in the crook of her shoulder. Some women were too tall or too short for him to do that comfortably, but she was just right. Kayla had many attributes that fit him well. She had just enough adventure to take some chances in her daily life, like the weekend at his home, but cautious enough to weigh her decision before making it.

"I took some time to look at examples of your work over the last months. I'm impressed with your eye for detail. Your photos tell the story with little need for words. Impressive talent."

She stepped through the elevator door. River placed a keycard against the sensor and punched in a code.

"Um, security an issue?"

"Nope."

A car had pulled in behind them a distance away, and without saying anything, he watched to see if they exited, and if not, why not?

"You noticed them too?"

"Them?"

"The windows are tinted, but the front driver's window must stay see-thru. I saw a passenger. Don't know about the back, of course."

River never slowed but hit the close door mechanism. They rode up in silence.

"Good observation skills."

"They can come in handy, now did you not know those people?"

"No, and they didn't have a sticker in the window saying they are authorized to park on this level. Visitors park on the lower level for safety. They must go through the lobby to be allowed to the elevators. That's not to say they aren't here with someone else who is authorized."

"So, how do you think they got to the residents' level?"

"Not a clue, but I intend to find out." He picked up a phone and spoke to someone. "Collier, we have an unidentified silver BMW on the resident level without a sticker. Can you check that out? Thanks."

"Who was that?"

"My parents' bodyguard."

"They have a bodyguard?"

"Yep. They've had one for years out of necessity. Collier has been with them for close to twenty years. My sister is pregnant now, and she has a bodyguard companion. Jacob insists on it. He runs the exporting part of the business, and he is often in places he can't get to his phone or even hear it. His assistant is pretty good, but Chandra is busy herself and can't worry about someone wanting to abduct her or cause trouble."

"Chandra is your sister? I never met her at the Gala."

"No, she runs the accounting department and oversees human resources. We have over three hundred employees, so until the baby is born or she says she's had enough, she is at the helm and vulnerable. She's also exempt from fancy dress."

Kayla laughed. "I get it. Now, who's your bodyguard?"

He gave her an exaggerated offended face. "I don't need a bodyguard. You, on the other hand, do."

She ignored the second half of his statement. "Why don't you need one?"

"I can handle myself. When I'm ninety, I'll hire one."

"Even if you aren't paying attention because you are hard at work?"

"Even then. But you—"

"Wow, are you at the top?" exclaimed Kayla. "This is a spectacular view."

"I get the message and will let this go for now. No, my parents are on the top floor. Chandra and I have the 19th floor."

"You live with your sister?"

"Yes and no. Come in, and I'll be able to explain better if you are looking at the set up at the same time."

River knew the entrance was grand with the Seattle skyline displayed through the windows. It really was spectacular. Evidently, Kayla thought so too.

"This is magnificent, but you know that, don't you?"

"I do. It is nice on a clear day. A little harder on days when the fog is heavy. You feel as though you are alone in the world. A bit unsettling if you are first waking up, which is why I draw the curtains at night. Come in here."

He led her into the long, broad common room. "We use this space for entertaining mostly, but it's technically the living room. As you can see, the dining area and kitchen area combine with the large living area making up the home center, which creates the main living space. There are two wings. Mine is on the left and Chandra's on the right. We have our own homes, and we both go home usually, but when the situation demands more, we stay here. Chandra's husband, Jacob, is a stickler about the rules. She can't drive tired or hungry, especially now that she's pregnant."

Kayla's voice mellowed. "He must really love her."

"He does. Chandra doesn't always appreciate his way of showing it."

Kayla sat on the closest sofa with a sigh. "I understand that sentiment."

"Yes, I bet you do. Please, make yourself at home."

Kayla jumped up. "Oh, I'm sorry. I shouldn't have—"

"Honey, I meant for you to please, make yourself at home, not to call attention to the fact that you sat without invitation. You were here having wild, monkey sex with me last night and left from here this morning. When I'm in my own private surroundings, I don't feel anyone with me is a guest. I don't invite people to my inner sanctums unless they are friends or family. I have a limited amount of either category. You are here. Therefore you are welcome to do what makes you comfortable."

Kayla sat down hesitantly. "You're sure?"

"Kayla." He loaded chastisement and attitude, and so much more into that word.

"Okay. So, if that's true, do you have any Bailey's? I love it warmed."

"No, but I have the ingredients to make you an Irish Cream if that's what you want."

"Oh, I wouldn't put you out. I'll take anything but beer. I hate the stuff. Pee water is what it tastes to me."

River laughed. "It's no bother, but on the beer, you must not have tasted any microbrews or the good stuff. I bet we could find a tasty one you'd like."

"I doubt it. I don't like Guinness, and my father said I was hopeless."

"Nah, that's an acquired taste. There are plenty of others. Now, I'll make your hot toddy, and you pick out some music. Nothing too energetic because tonight we're teasing out the things that tell us you were targeted on your last trip. I want to be clear, no matter what we come up with and avenues of investigation we open up, this absolutely does not mean it's okay to go back. It's just to see if we can trace the person and take care of that problem happening again."

"You aren't going to hurt him, right?"

"Or her? Nope, but we need to know and turn the person into the authorities. Preferably ours."

As they sat on the couch with their respective drinks, River picked pressed a remote, and a smart screen lowered from the ceiling. "What's this?"

"A screen that I use to do my strategy and thinking work. It types what I say. Then I delete what I don't want and keep the rest. It is connected to a computer system and doesn't lose anything."

"Wow, you're intense."

"You should try it. Here, let's start." He hit the remote again, and the screen's message read, 'Ready when you are River.'

"Kayla's trip to Africa: What went wrong? Draft 1." The words appeared on the heading.

"Now, let's go over all the things that were off about your trip. Ready?" River loved he could share this method with Kayla. He imagined most women to not be interested.

"Yes. Turn it on. Number one: Flights were changed without prior notice or discussion."

"Number two..."

They had a long list of abnormalities that had there been only one or two, it would have been a coincidence but put all together, it was disturbing.

"That's all I can do tonight," declared Kayla after nearly an hour. "That is an impressive piece of work we did. Your method is incredible." The silence in the pause became awkward.

"It's not too late. If you're interested, we could watch the city for a while. I love to do that on a clear night. It helps me unwind."

"Um, sure. That'd be nice."

He settled them on another sofa, bringing a soft blanket out of the coffee table storage compartment. "This will help you relax. What do you have on for tomorrow?"

"Not a whole lot. Polishing my next piece, mostly."

"Good. Stay the night. I promise to get you home in the morning. I'll leave you to work while I finish some things, and if you aren't done by the time three o'clock rolls around, you can bring it with you. I promise I have everything you'll need to finish."

She paused. "I'm not sure."

River knew it was a bold move, but his desire for this woman had resurfaced hard in the last several days. Tonight, he could think of nothing else but to take her, love her, and protect her for much longer than one night. Hard as it was, he waited Kayla out as she thought. River nearly laughed at the mental conversation it was obvious she was having with herself.

He kissed the top of her head. When she leaned into him, he took the advantage and did it again, bringing his hands into play. Carefully massaging her shoulders, then kissing where he soothed. River continued, kneading her muscles, caressing her skin, and placing his lips over the relaxed areas. When he had run out of accessible parts, he was about to start over when Kayla turned her head and lifted it as she reached up to tug his neck closer, bringing his lips down to hers.

A little shifting and River allowed Kayla to straddle his waist, giving her control. He'd take it back soon enough, but right now, she needed it. The girl was intense, and meeting her stroke for stroke became all-consuming. Her tongue came out tentatively at first, but when he sucked on it, she seemed to explode with desire. Hands were touching, feeling, caressing both exposed and covered body parts.

Suddenly, it appeared that Kayla needed more than that. She sat up, pulling her dress over her head and where it landed was anyone's guess. Her bra went flying next. Thankful Chandra was home and not at the condo tonight, he shivered when he felt a hot, wet tongue on his chest. The enchantress sat on his rib cage and continue to move south very quickly, opening his clothing, helping herself to his tingling belly. His cock was straining to be unleashed on her glistening pussy. It left a wet trail as she inched down his body. His cock fucking hurt. Now her pussy was nearly over his cock still in his slacks. Time to take over.

Rolling Kayla over on her back, she protested with little moans and mews. His breath was coming as hard, and as fast as hers was. Time to hit the bedroom before things happened in the front room. Not that he minded, but he thought she wouldn't want to be reminded of their hot session without boundaries every time she entered the condo, and she would be entering often. Later, she wouldn't care, but he was trying to think of her with the last moments of cognitive, sane thought he possessed.

Scooping her up in nothing but slick, wet panties, which he immediately stripped off her, River strode, half-clothed, into the bedroom. The city skyline and ambiance went unnoticed. Placing her gently in the center of the bed with little more than a bounce on landing, he stripped down to his skin. Opening the side drawer, he pulled out a few condoms and, tearing one open, he rolled the ribbed latex on.

His knee pressed down beside her, keeping his eyes on her. Kayla licked her lips and held out her hands. Her breasts were soft, bouncy, and firm as he palmed them before taking one peaked nipple in his mouth. Her reaction was gratifying. This woman was on fire, and she drew him into the flames with her. One breast, then another, he suckled, feeling the light scraping of her nails down his back to his buttocks, the heat from her hands retracing the scorching lines she'd laid.

Kayla's voice was raspy. "I need to feel you. Come inside, River, please."

Her breath was labored, shallow, rapid, her skin as sweaty as his and God, he needed to surround himself in her slick heat as much as she needed him to take her. He pushed her thighs apart with his knees as he rose between her legs. She widened them to give him room to settle between those tanned, creamy thighs.

"Okay, sweetheart. Here I am."

Even with the latex encasing his staff and the extra texture, he could feel her heat and feel the slickness as he slowly slid inside. Trying to go carefully, as a gentleman should, he nearly lost his balance when she grabbed his forearms and, in one smooth move, wrapped her legs around his waist and slammed her pelvis into his.

He chuckled. He got her message. He'd yet to touch her clit and knew he should, but she was slamming him hard. Time to take back the control. He leaned down over her face and kissed her hard.

"My turn. Touch your clit." She shook her head. "Don't need to, just do it. I'm one of the lucky ones. You proved that last night."

"Let's see what else I can prove, shall we?"

Pounding into her, she seemed to crave the roughness that he had not wanted to give her. She ground her hips against him. He felt her clit making contact with his pelvis, likely giving her all she needed. Kayla was growing frantic, he was feeling the low pressure in his spine, and his pelvis built rapidly into a ball of fire. God he loved that feeling. Kayla was arching, her climax within seconds.

Soon the valve was released, and leaning on his knees again, he placed his hand between her body and his, one tweaking her breast, one flicking her clit as he moved. She shot like the proverbial rocket. Kayla lay frozen in time momentarily before making the friction between them again as she rode out her release. He followed her, his own body making its sounds and motions of orgasmic pleasure.

River tweaked her nipples one last time, made a caressing round of his finger on her hard, hot clit, and rolled her over on his belly so he could indulge a little longer in her heat around his cock. Finally, knowing she needed to get some of the sweat off her and her own slickness washed, he kissed her lips. She took up the challenge and kissed until they were both breathless again.

"Sorry, baby. I need to take care of the condom and get you a washcloth. You're so flushed."

She simply made an unintelligible sound of understanding and rolled next to him in the bed. Her hand reached down to thread her fingers in his pubic hair, closing them in a fist. No one had ever done that before. It was familiar and sensual, and hot as hell. The spirit was willing, but he needed a couple more minutes before attempting to make sweet love to her. First things first.

Coming back into the room, he reached down to open her legs just a little more and found Kayla to be fast asleep. He pushed one leg out, and she unconsciously spread them. He thought she was awake at first, but as he freshened her, she let out a very soft snore. He smiled.

Kissing her red, well-used mouth, he pulled the sheet out from under her and drew her to him, his chin resting on the top of her head. They'd move in the night, but right now, this was heaven. This woman had sucked him in without even trying. He was so screwed, and for the first time in his life, he wasn't looking for the exit.

Chapter Nine

Late the next afternoon, Kayla was waiting for River to pick her up. He apologized.

"I'm so sorry, baby. Something has come up, and I didn't want to have to deal with it over our weekend."

Kayla was a little relieved because it meant she could get in and gather her clothes during the end of week meeting that Sarge held for the Company. She didn't need, nor was she interested in being a part of the gathering. It would have been a different story if he had let her onto the playing field, but since hell hadn't frozen over yet, she could safely give them a miss.

As she sat in her apartment, she thought back what the last forty-eight hours had brought her. In a word, River. Who would have known a kidnapping and a home-cooked meal would have put so many other things in play. Dinner was good, the strategy session was invigorating and educational. River's mind was the proverbial steel trap when it came to detail, cause, and affect.

And then the sex, well, she was aroused just thinking about it. River didn't pressure Kayla to perform or share equally in the act. In fact, there was no doubt about the fact that he was waiting her out. He was quietly tender as she spent precious minutes debating whether she was making a mistake or not. To be honest, there was no buyer's remorse on her part. What about his? Did he push the flight back, thinking he didn't want to pursue this budding thing they had started? Maybe he wasn't as attracted to her as she was to him.

She'd texted him midday, but there was no response. Was it possible he really did only date a woman once, like Gunner had said? But that wasn't it, they had spent two nights together, and he said he never brought women home. Maybe he wished he hadn't committed to the weekend. Now what?

Her phone dinged. Wasn't that pathetic? She had already given him his own designated notification ping and ring tone, and he didn't want to see her again? She glanced at her phone, recognizing her father's notification tone. Dinner? No, even if she wasn't going away with River for the weekend, she didn't want her family's company tonight.

Kayla reached for her suitcase and turned to unload the clothing in the spacious closet the apartment held. It was nearly the size of the rest of the apartment. The tears slowly streaked down her face. She let them. What else could she do? Her phone beeped again. This time it was River's melody, I Don't Want to Miss a Thing, by Aerosmith. More damn tears. She swiped at them hard.

"Hello." There was silence. This was it. Well, she could save him the trouble and her pride. "Riv—"

"Kayla," he said simultaneously. "Are you ready, honey? Sorry I've been unavailable today and running late. Do I need to come up to help you? Hold on. Let me park."

She sniffed and smiled. "No, I'm... ah, I finished my work, so it's just a suitcase. I'm coming down now."

She hadn't told her father she would be gone for the weekend. She'd text him at the airport. She smiled at River, and he gave her a kiss as he put her and her suitcase in the car. He hesitated but didn't say anything.

As they pulled out into traffic, he said, "What's wrong."

"Nothing." Damn, was that too perky?

"Mmm hm. Try again unless you want me to guess."

"What, no, I mean, it's just been a long day."

"Do long days make you cry?"

"Sometimes?"

"You thought because I didn't respond to your texts and didn't call you, then you got the notification that the flight was changed, that I had changed my mind."

"Well, I guess I thought we'd connected. That's okay. I mean, I understand you're a one date kind of guy."

His eyes stayed on the road, but his hand patted her thigh. "You're right, I have never dated a woman twice. And you are right about us connecting. We all change, and this is me doing just that. I want this weekend, maybe more than you because that was the kind of person I have always been: a one and done. You made me want to change that. You're the only woman that made me interested in chucking that lifestyle out the window."

"But you didn't the first time we were together. At the first Foundation benefit."

"Didn't what, pursue you? Change my ways? Honey, you were twenty-one. I left before we did anything more than turn on the burner. We never had a chance to cook. Things like this take time; they have to simmer. I didn't have that kind of luxury. Now I do."

She laughed. "So, are we cooking now?"

"You had better believe it. Here we are. I'm going to let you off at the gate. You should have gotten a copy of our ticket. Check us in at the kiosk. I don't have a bag, and you can carry that little case on."

"Where are you going?"

"Parking. You need to learn to trust me. I have no intention of leaving you stranded."

"I do. I mean, I'm working on it. You're still new."

"I get it. We'll get there. Just promise me that until we do, you will ask when you have concerns or questions instead of jumping to conclusions."

"I can do that." She hopped out of the car to start the check-in process.

IT WASN'T DARK YET. The remnants of the sun's rays reflected on a glorious vision of snow-capped mountains, sparkling ocean, and green forests as they landed at the tiny international airport. The incredible view encompassed everything, and Kayla was excited. The entire environment was teaming with life. Boats, floatplanes, cars, people, and she was sure there were ocean life and wildlife everywhere as well.

"It's amazing! I mean, there's an eagle! No, two, three! Is that a cruise ship?"

"Yes, we get the odd one or five during the summer days." His grin was relaxed and indulgent.

"I'm sorry."

"For what? I love that you're excited. I can get complacent after seeing it day after day, but I love my home."

"Who wouldn't? I mean, I did research, so I knew all of this was here. We have these things in Seattle, but not like this. This is immersion."

River laughed as he unbuckled her seat belt and stood to grab her bag from the overhead compartment. "Yes, and when it rains, it feels like you are immersed, all right."

A man slapped River on the upper arm. She watched as he schooled his irritation behind his inquiring look. "River, glad you're home. I need to talk to you about something. You busy tomorrow?"

"Joe." River said as he reached out his hand. "Actually, I am. I'll be available Tuesday, though. Call Karen to make an appointment. I'll tell her to look for your call. Or shoot her an email."

Joe looked around River and spied Kayla. "A new associate?"

"No, this is Kayla, my companion."

Companion? Huh. Clearly, Joe didn't know what to do with that designation either because he half smiled at her and shook her hand. "Tuesday, then," he said as they faced forward to wait their turn to unload.

River nodded. "See you then."

As Joe walked off ahead, River guided her through the emptying aisle and off the plane. Once in his truck, he turned and said, "If I had said you were my girlfriend, he would have been on the phone telling our business to the world. Your name and probably a grainy photo would have appeared on a thousand phones before we even finished dinner. This way, it was the truth without making anyone go crazy."

"Would it really be that bad?"

He laughed mirthlessly. "Without a doubt. Tomorrow the number would be untold. The whole island would be trying to get a look at you. When the time is right, I'll make a formal announcement, but I think our families should hear it first, don't you?"

All she could do was stare at River. "You mean to declare me as your girlfriend?"

"Too soon?" he asked, a small but obvious grin playing about his mouth.

"Isn't it?"

He shrugged. "Not for me."

"Oh." And why did that fill her up with liquid warmth?

The tone for the rest of the weekend was set, which turned out to be just as entertaining and beautiful as the arrival. The weather held. River was all business when someone would stop him and discuss something serious. He commanded attention when they went to a community summer staple, a play called "Seining for Love on Dry Land and Wet Rocks." It was about the perils of a lonely fisherman making a living on his seiner he called Dry Land. She figured out that the 'wet rocks' was Cache Island, and he tried to find his true love. It was a delightful comedy, and dinner accompanied the play. The fisherman discovered his true love where he least expected her—in the saloon.

In the evening, as they watched television or sat and talked, River was a gentleman. He didn't even try to take her to bed to do more than sleep the first night, but by the wee hours of the morning, her adventuresome kisses had changed his mind. Thankfully, it set the tone for the remainder of the bedtime ritual.

"I'm going to be with you the way I am. This is me in a relationship." Kayla smiled. He was too accommodating for him to be this way always, but it would do for now. If he wanted her to fall for him, it was working. She loved her time with him.

All too soon, it was time to leave the totems, bears, whales, seals, and eagles behind. Oh, and the gossips. River had been right. His little island paradise was full of them. Regardless, her weekend with a thoughtful lover and conscientious host was incredible. He teased her by day and night. They played hard during the day and harder at night.

As Kayla entered the airport screening line, her chest felt constricted when she had to say goodbye. She suddenly didn't want to go, not if he was staying. It was hard to leave the beauty and almost impossible to leave River. She knew that he had work to do and that the weekend they shared was like a mini-vacation where you try your best to push the rest of the world out, but she wanted to see him every day. Her nose was tingling with unreleased tears. How did a man do that to you when you least expected it?

"I'm sorry, sweetheart, but I have a weekend seminar this coming week. Can I swing by and grab you Sunday night and bring you home?"

"I can't. I have a three-day class to teach. Will you call me?"

"Damn. Yes, we'll video chat. It's your turn in line, baby. Call me when you get home. No, when you land."

"Okay."

"Okay."

She turned to the screener, and when she turned back, River was gone. And there were those stupid tears again.

Sarge met her at the door when she returned home. When she looked up into her father's stern face, Kayla remembered what she'd forgotten: to notify her family she would be gone for the weekend.

And keeping her phone off for the whole three days and nights obviously didn't go over too well with her over-protective father.

"Hi, dad. Before you say it, I'm sorry. I was going to call, then got busy and never thought of it again. I'm an adult. Well past the age of needing to ask permission. But I am sorry if I worried you."

"*If* you worried me? Who were you with?" He asked as he moved to allow her inside.

She expected more fanfare before getting to this question. She thought about saying no one, but if Sarge mentioned it to River, that man would have spilled the beans. "River."

"Bennett? Why?"

"Excuse me? He took me to his place on Cache Island. It's beautiful, especially when the sun is out."

"Did he say he would sign on and help with some of the heavier projects?"

"Nope. We didn't talk about it. And before you say it, there was no reason to discuss any of your work. You've made it more than plain that I have no business in this company except if I want to be your errand girl, so I don't care if he helps or not."

"Kayla Rhea, that is not—"

"Save it, Sarge. I'm tired. I'm taking a hot shower and going to bed. I have a full week of prepping for a three-day seminar, so don't expect to see me much these next days."

"With River?"

"No, with students and people of the community. I do still teach, you know. I'm also doing a small first showing of my photos for the next series of articles." Sarge followed Kayla into the kitchen and waited until she poured herself a glass of juice before asking questions again.

"What photos? You didn't stay there last time. You remember the time you were kidnapped?" His sarcasm rolled off Kayla. She knew he'd been worried, and it was her fault.

"I seem to recall that incident." She couldn't keep her own irritation out of her response. "You know, I've always thought how odd that my camera, tablet, and phone survived the kidnapping. I've never figured that out since neither the men in our benevolent group nor the police said they never caught the driver or found the taxi. They were all in my backpack that I was forced to leave behind at the airport. The items I left in the vehicle when we stopped. Good thing I had my hip pack."

Sarge's tone became more contemplative. "That is strange."

"Right? And yet, they were all gathered when I checked inside the bag that they returned to me before I boarded the plane."

All Sarge did was grunt. Men. She knew it was a sore subject with him that they never found the people. She stopped musing aloud.

"So, you and Bennett?"

"Are friends. I don't know if we will ever be more than that, but I like him as a person. I'm going to bed."

"It's early."

"I didn't get a lot of sleep this weekend."

Sarge grunted again before letting her leave the kitchen. It was hours before she fell asleep, thinking of the weekend and her feelings for one surprising former SEAL.

The next morning, as Kayla put a cold compress on her tired, swollen eyes, she wondered why Sarge was grinning from ear to ear. She knew she would likely regret the question, but she asked it anyway.

"What's got you so happy?"

"River Bennett called me last night. He's accepted. Why are your eyes so red?"

She tried to keep her physical reaction to hearing his name to a minimum. No use giving away her feelings to the menfolk. They had enough ammunition they didn't hesitate to use on her. It would open up River to extra aggravation. Besides, it had only been a weekend. She missed him. It'd be another week before she would see him. What could she tell Sarge? Allergies. That was perfect.

"Allergies. That's nice that River called. I understand he keeps pretty busy, so I hope you don't think that he means more than very occasionally."

"Doesn't matter because that is all I would need him for, and he knows that." Kayla nodded as she let him continue. "He said he'd help with the occasional job from the com-center. Then I called his friend on the joint command base up there, and he said he'd appreciate the help if they had a rescue that needed extra men, but we'd have to go through their course. I'm not as young as I once was, but the boys, they'd enjoy it.

"Taren maybe, but probably not Robbie."

"Well, Taren and the rest would be having a heyday."

"Good for them, dad. I have to go. I'll try to stop by sometime this week, but I think I'll just stay in town. I have to concentrate on the workshop I'm putting on."

"If you think you need to, we will miss you."

"You'll miss my cooking, you mean."

"That too," Sarge said with a grin. "Oh, before you go, River said you left something when you went home yesterday. He wants you to call him."

"Really, I wonder what I left?" Sarge grunted but didn't answer. It was becoming his standard with her when he was trying to avoid an argument.

Later that afternoon, happy with her progress in tweaking her first day's presentation, Kayla made herself a sandwich and flipped open her university email. She weeded through the typical announcements and reminders, along with a few inquiries about her workshop. After cleaning the rest out as clutter, she noticed one with a subject line, "Death in Somalia."

Suddenly she was shaking with the cold icy fingers of fear coming up from her belly and wrapping her in a vice grip of panic. Self-talk helped her through most things she had no control over, so Kayla tried to rationalize the fear she was holding. It wasn't the first communication she had concerning Africa, but it may have been the first to mention death and Somalia together. And Kayla did not give out her Uni email address except for those things concerning the college. Still shaking and battling an overwhelming sense of dread, but more curious than worried for her safety, she clicked on the message.

It was a photo, nothing odd or strange about it. Nothing threatening or compromising, simply a photo of her on the tarmac in Somalia. River was standing next to her, in what looked like a protective stance. She was growing familiar with that body language and the message it sent. As she studied the photo for something that should stand out to her, she realized the situation captured in the picture was the odd thing about it.

Only a few people were there when she boarded the plane. It had to be one of them who took the photo. Kayla didn't remember anyone snapping a picture. She looked at the email and saw nothing but numbers, and the domain seemed private. Robbie would know about this. She'd send it to him. If she knew who sent it, she might then understand why.

The next photo was considerably different. It was so shocking, it took time to mentally process what she was looking at. The scene before her showed a bloody, dead woman whose body had been left to bloat. It was partially eaten by animals. The fact that it was a woman was unrecognizable except for two things. The female clothing was limiting the expansion of the decomposition gases held inside the body. The undeniable likeness of Kayla's face superimposed on it.

The message read, "Africa can be a dangerous country, especially for those who don't know how to keep their mouths shut."

The room grew hot, Kayla's breathing became labored, her hands cold. Nausea came in overpowering waves, and she didn't know if she could get to the bathroom before she ejected the bile. Stumbling over the side of the chair, she nearly landed on the floor. The wall held her weakening body as she slid along it to get to the toilet. For long moments, Kayla released her stomach contents and then continued to dry heave when there was nothing else to spew. Finally, exhausted, she cleaned what she could see and laid down on the sofa to recover.

Kayla woke to her phone ringing and the door knocking hard. "Kayla, are you okay, baby?"

Familiar and yet unidentifiable in her fuzzy awakening brain, Kayla laid there without answering either summons. Finally, she looked at the phone that had stopped ringing and saw River's name on the I.D. of multiple missed calls. She heard his voice.

"River?" her raw throat released little sound. The table made a loud, scraping sound as she bumped it with her leg. She cried out. The knocking became pounding.

"Kayla, open the door, honey."

"River."

She made it to the door and opened it, falling onto his chest without warning. He wrapped her in his arms and lifted. She had a second's thought to protest, but she needed him as close as she could get him as the events of the afternoon resurfaced on her brain. River brought her back inside, pausing to check out the small apartment before kicking the door shut behind him and walking them to the sofa she had just left.

He held her for a moment longer before sitting her down on the leather-covered cushion, "What's going on? What's happened? Are you sick?"

She looked away. "I didn't get much sleep last night. Why do you think something has happened?"

His bark of frustrated disbelief singed her ears. "Because I called you more times than I can remember and pounded on your door calling your name for at least four or five minutes. This is a small place, so you had to have heard me. I'm sure we will have the police showing up soon.

Just be kind and tell them I was worried about you. I'm not a crazy man trying to steal your virtue."

"If you want me to, but could you be him just a little?"

"Later." He sighed and shook his head. "Now, talk. What has gone on here?"

"Nothing, I just took a nap and must have slept hard."

"Take sleeping pills?"

"What? No, I never do."

"Then, I know that something happened because you look exhausted, and you woke up easily when we were at my house, despite the late nights."

"Maybe I didn't want to miss anything."

"Kayla." He did it to her again. The amount of meaning he conveyed in calling her name like that was incredible, and she had a hard time not caving in, but she was stronger than that. She had to be.

"I have to go to the bathroom, please. You'll need to let me up. What time is it?"

"Six-thirty. I'm calling for delivery, and you go to the bathroom."

"No fish. I have that on Wednesdays when I'm here. The best fish special is at the market on Wednesday. Oh, and can mine be a little bland. My stomach was off earlier today."

"You weren't well?"

"You could say that." With that, she got up and detoured by the desk to click the screen off. No need to have that still up when she opened the computer. She would get a copy to Robbie and go from there.

She was washing her hands when River's "Holy Hell" could be heard loudly. He must have found it. Damn it. Why didn't she have a password on her computer? He was too observant.

River appeared at the bathroom door, and Kayla tried to divert the conversation she knew he wanted to have. "Good thing I grew up with little private space, or I'd be upset you are in the bathroom with me."

His face was grim. "Technically, I am at the door, not inside. But that, young lady, is the least of your worries. Where the hell did that email come from?" His tone was quiet and intense, like Sarge's when he was emotional.

"No idea." She took a shaky breath. "It just appeared in my inbox. I don't want you to worry about it. I'll call Robbie."

River watched Kayla for a moment, and as he suspected, he sensed no guile. After the weekend, he had a pretty good handle on her now, and he didn't think she lacked attention. No, this email was real. And the threat was real. His protective instincts were operating in overdrive, just as they had when he heard she was the one who had been kidnapped.

River Bennett had been running his world in its entirety for over fifteen years, living on his own for twenty. When he returned to civilian life, however, his world of influence had expanded. Once River returned to the family engineering business, his own father, Jon Bennett, Jr., was still at the height of his game. So, at thirty-seven, River took over as head of the Bennett Family Foundation using his degrees and military training. It was gratifying to work with just enough challenge to keep him busy.

Everything changed when his father had a stroke six months later. Jon's stroke, from which he fully recovered, showed the fifty-seven-year-old, he needed more corporate help from River and a few more department heads. River stepped in to help run the business with his sister. She was great at accounting, but the people part would never be her thing even though she was also the Human Resources overseer. It wasn't his either, but being diplomatic in the military was one thing you learned fast in ops. Who said grunts couldn't find a job in the 'real' world?

He turned his eyes back to her questioning ones. They had to take this as a serious threat. She couldn't stay alone for right now. "I need to put in a call to Zayden, and we need to let your father know."

"I know. Can we just wait until after my seminar on the weekend? Otherwise, he isn't going to let me do it. The access points are too many, and he will connect the University email to the University seminar and stop me."

He followed her back to the main room. "That's the most logical conclusion."

"Maybe, but Robbie says that there are all kinds of ways to make something appear different than it is in the computer and internet world."

"Understood, but we can't disregard that it is as it seems. It would be irresponsible to allow you to go to the seminar without an escort. Protection of some kind. And we would want the ways in and out of the room to be minimized and covered. That will take a few days of mobilization."

"I'm fine. I promise."

She hated the pleading in her voice, but she'd lived with men like the one standing in front of her, and she had seen River when he had his mind set on something. Begging wasn't difficult when she knew it would take that.

"We might be able to compromise, but that's it. Let me make my calls, and then I'll tell you what I can and will do and what I won't do."

She lowered her voice and said, "You can't force me to do what you want."

He lowered his voice to match hers, his words resonated along her skin, bringing a tingle. "Don't challenge me on this, Kayla. I will do what is best for you. Full stop. And you will allow me to take care of you. Understood?" His hand came up and caressed her cheek. How should she respond to that gesture of tenderness, the look in his eyes that pleaded her to give over control?

Her throat closed around the words that were trapped inside. The part of herself that took pride in being the independent, self-sufficient woman of the world knew that she needed help in the face of this type of threat. She should hate that the reality was she wanted River to deal with this, and yet, she didn't. She engaged in all sorts of battles to retain her autonomy in her testosterone-filled world, but she almost welcomed the bravado in this instance. All she could do was nod in response to River, or she would lose the fight to keep her tears at bay.

River smiled, further gentling his demeanor and losing his intensity. He answered her nod with a tilt of his head as he lowered his lips to hers. Hoovering just above her, he whispered, "Thank you, baby," before giving her a kiss she couldn't think through. His lips touched hers, suspending all cognitive abilities as she gave in to the kiss. His tongue engaged hers in a duel, teasing and taunting, circling and jabbing, establishing his dominance. She needed the reassurance, the unconditional acceptance. She needed him to want her. If his kiss was any indication, he did.

He mimicked the mating dance and pulled back with a sigh, placing his forehead on hers in a declaration of intimacy. "It's going to be all right. We will take care of this, but I need you to stay at home or my place until we figure it out. Staying here is not an option."

"I can lock the doors. I work better when there isn't a gang of antsy ex-military all around me."

"Then come home with me. I'm the only previous military member at the condo. After this weekend, we will know more and can reassess."

"River."

"No, this is what I do best. I ask the right questions, get the right intel, and then make a plan based on my understanding of the situation. It's what I do, Kayla. Let me do it."

"Okay."

"Okay. I'll start the calls. You gather everything you'll need. I'll have to get you another computer because this one is going to Robbie. I doubt it will help much, but any direction is good. Is this the first email like this you've ever received?"

"Yes."

"So, no threatening emails, no nasty grams from people who don't like what you do?"

"Well, of course, I have, but nothing like this. Typically, it's people who say women shouldn't go to those places. Or we have no right to impose our thinking on other cultures. They say rude things about the girls' morals, my morals, that I'm stirring up trouble, all that. But nothing violent. This is very violent and a direct threat."

"And what does Sarge say about these emails?"

"He doesn't know. Why would I worry him like that?"

"And why jeopardize your chance of continuing to go back?"

"Yes."

"Kayla, this is the end of you keeping these emails to yourself."

She flung her hand in frustration. "I know. This is the first one from inside the university. The others were easy to trace or were just hot air. This one..."

"This one upped the ante." River was back to business. "Gather your things."

He turned away, in no doubt Kayla would do as he said, but she'd already agreed, hadn't she? It was rather self-evident that going to his condo was not a good idea, but she was going anyway. He excited her physically and mentally. Emotionally was a different story. After seeing how depraved man could be to his own kind, Kayla wasn't eager to give someone that intimate part of herself.

RIVER HAD NO IDEA WHAT brought on the sudden email because it had been a year since she'd been kidnapped, a year since she'd been in-country. Yes, she had done a few interviews, but that was a few months ago since the last one. She'd taught two classes the previous semester, but not one this semester. She hadn't done much but work during the first six months after arriving home. River hadn't asked her yet, but he imagined she was recovering mentally. So, what triggered the email? The seminar? And if that was it, why not the classes?

"Is that you, River?"

"Yep, and I have Kayla here with me. Can you hold on a minute?" He held the cell against his chest and said, "Kayla, I need a roster of those signed up to take your seminar. Send a copy to Robbie, then shut down the computer." He went back to Taren. "Okay, we have a situation that you need to keep under your hat until I get to Sarge. I'll explain when I get there, but I'm bringing Kayla from the apartment to get some clothes."

"What the hell does she need more clothes for?"

"Wait until we get there. I need Robbie to start checking this list of people signed up for Kayla's seminar. She's sending it shortly. I need to know if there is anything we should know about them. Subversive? Protestors, sympathizers, records, the whole shebang. Also, could you find out if that benevolent group of Kayla's have gone back since the incident? Male and female participants. Any repeats? We'll be there soon." He disconnected.

"Got everything, baby? Remember, you aren't coming back, but if you find you did miss something, I'll get Taren or someone else to retrieve it for you."

"It was just an email."

"At the very least, it was an act of intimidation. At the very most, it was a warning of things to come. I don't intend on either of those things to escalate." The apartment was shut down, the lights turned off, the deadbolt was locked. River put her packs on her and him, gathered her other cases, and they went to the car.

As they loaded the back of his SUV with her seminar items, a young man called to her. He looked to be early to mid-twenties. River went into immediate protection mode, tossing the bags in the back and engulfing her in his presence.

"Hi, Jared," said Kayla as she passed River an irritated look. Too damn bad. Kayla stepped around him as she smiled broadly at the young man. "Are you still coming to the seminar?"

"I'd planned on it. I hope I'm not called in to cover a shift. I need the credit."

"Then don't answer your phone for the weekend."

"If only it were that simple. But yes, I expect to be there."

"Great. I'll see you then."

"Hey, wait, I thought you were at the apartment until the weekend. I had hoped to discuss some things." He looked at River who's demeanor left him with no illusions about whether he was annoyed or not.

"We'll have time at the seminar. I'll see you then," called Kayla as River began herding her to the front of the vehicle.

"Are you sure you're all right? I mean," Jared tilted his head in River's direction.

"Oh, he wouldn't hurt a fly or me."

"Of course not," said an insulted River. He murmured under his breath, "but spanking is a whole other thing."

"Bye, Jared." The young man walked away hesitantly and looked back several times as though contemplating whether he should do anything about River or not. River was spoiling for a fight, but he didn't have time right now. More's the pity. Oh well. He reached over and buckled her seat belt."

"I can do that myself. I'm not a child."

"No, but you're sure naughty, so just settle down, and we'll have you home in no time."

River had no intention of allowing Kayla to brush this email off as she had evidently done before. The timing was shit. He had his planning weekend, and as much as he needed to become fully immersed in that part of his life for a few days, River also knew he couldn't do it if he didn't trust her protection. It would've been easier if he could have left her with his parents or Chandra and Jacob, but Kayla had her own commitments. As much as he loved that she was her own woman and not needy, it also made for a very difficult workaround in times like this. A bodyguard sounded good right about now.

His first call went to Robert Rhea. "River, sorry about not getting that paperwork to you yet. I've been handed another mess I'm untangling. I'll get it to you soon."

River took a deep breath. They were not in a dire situation, and he could take the extra minute or two to reiterate his position with Sarge before demanding the things he needed from that same group of people. His impatience at explaining himself at all was overpowering, but a necessity, and honestly, he was still waiting for Kayla. *Don't be an ass; build rapport.*

"You understand that I have the family's foundation to run, so I wouldn't often be available, maybe a couple times a year."

"I do, and that's why it would be occasional with me."

"Did you call Zayden?"

"I did. I plan on meeting with the commander the next time he swings down to Seattle. He did want some of our guys to train with them when they have a free spot. It has to be when it is open, not scheduled. Evidently, that can only be done by certain agencies and the Military."

"Yes, I was assigned at the center at the end of my tour. It was a good transition assignment and keeps my skills up and my hand in on the occasions they need more in the community."

"Great, get back with me, and I'll figure out this paperwork shit. I don't know why Kayla won't just take this all on for me. Damn, stubborn woman. She wants to do more than help us in the office. She demands to be in those same places we are trying to keep her out of."

"Yes, sir, speaking of which, can I get a quick chat with your son, Rob?"

"Rob? Yes, I suppose. I, well hold on, here's his number." River thanked him and called Robbie.

"Hey, this is River. We have a situation that I need you to keep under your hat until I get there to sit down with Sarge and explain it in person. Kayla got an email today."

Chapter Ten

Kayla looked at the last of the four-part article she'd written and sighed. She entertained mixed emotions on this one. She loved that she could tell the story, but it left her with many unresolved feelings. It wasn't about her brothers' warnings or even her father's edict. How could she not go back if things were getting worse? The girls needed a loud, universal voice, but the email had shaken her.

She sighed and printed a finalized copy she would later send to the Journalistic News Magazine. They had promised her quite a bonus for this article and the exclusive on the kidnapping. That would give her more money to buy supplies when the time came to return. She needed to find others who couldn't afford the exclusive but wanted a piece of the work. Part of her was scared, a healthy emotion. The other part was terrified. That was not an emotion that was beneficial at all.

While there were many loving village communities, the region was deadly. This area was riddled with the devaluation of human life, rife with low survival rates due to poverty and high violence. People died for no more than being seen as an annoyance on another person's part. How could anyone feel they wanted that to continue? Evidently, someone did and was willing to communicate that desire to her in a threatening way.

River had no intention of letting her go without a full entourage of bodyguards, but she wasn't about to put up with that. What would her participants think of a person who said they went into these places but couldn't stand in a group of like-minded people in a safe environment with no less than three bodyguards? She knew what she would think.

She had put her foot down. With River, it was not as easy as one might have guessed, but he finally agreed on a two-man detail. She soon discovered he'd chosen her brothers.

"You might learn something, Taren," she half teased as little sisters would.

"Yeah, I'll tell you what I've learned so far. Your boyfriend tricked me into this by showing his strategic abilities. I'll get him back."

"River isn't my boyfriend. He's just a friend."

"Kayla, I might have been hoodwinked by your River, but I guarantee you, he is your boyfriend, significant other, whatever." Kayla shook her head and started to speak again. Taren placed his finger on her lips. "If you don't believe me, ask him. And until you do, don't contradict me." Brothers!

As the first day progressed and the first break came to a close, she spied Robbie in the lobby. He was listening and tapping away on the keyboard of a small set of laptops set up in the far corner. No one would be able to see what he was working on, but he was not hidden from view.

Robbie didn't seem to notice her as she approached his small operation. "Robert," she said in a hushed, angry tone. "What are you doing here?"

"Monitoring your email and other electronic access points. We're trying to see if you are being targeted by one of these people."

"It wasn't one of them."

"Don't be ignorant. You have no idea where it came from. We can act faster if we are here." He gentled his demeanor. "Look, Lala, I know that you are well able to take care of yourself, we all do, but you're ours. We would never forgive ourselves if we didn't take the precaution, and something happened that could have been prevented."

She sighed her capitulation. "Okay, but don't make anyone uncomfortable."

"Me? I'll just be in the corner here, doing my thing. Besides, I couldn't go anywhere because your boyfriend would hunt me down."

Just then, her phone rang. She saw there was a few moments before she needed to get back to her seminar students. "Hello?"

"Hey, honey. Things going well?"

"Yes, and how did you know this was my break?"

"I have the schedule. Rob sent it to me."

"You do know this is overkill, right?"

River's voice became serious. "No, what this is, is precautionary until we find out what happened last time you were in Africa, why you get these crazy emails, and why have they escalated. I'm not going to apologize, nor am I pulling anyone back."

"And do you know that my brothers think you are my boyfriend?" The last word was said in a stage whisper.

"I thought I was."

"Did you think to ask me?"

"Baby, I have to get back, and so do you. The permission part, I will apologize for. When are you done?"

"Check the schedule."

Kayla hung up and rushed to the bathroom. She needed to use the facilities and get back to her seminar. She pushed all thoughts, as crazy as they were, out of her mind. Walking back into the room, she saw most were sitting waiting to begin again. It didn't look like anyone had left out of boredom. Jared was there. Good.

Looking around the room one last time, she was gratified and, yes, needed to be part of a group of professionals who cared. She answered questions after her presentation and saw a journalist was amongst the participants. Odd. They weren't supposed to be there until the last day. She'd missed him the first time. He took a couple of photos, and she tried not to feel some trepidations. There was no reason to worry. But something was just off. She turned to answer a question.

"I heard you were kidnapped."

"True, and tomorrow I will tell you that story. Today let's focus on the need for these services. Groups like the one I worked with included nurses, teachers, and caregivers who trained the girls to come back from their despair. Giving the girls hope and options saved lives."

"Why do they need help if they're released?"

"Because no one else would help them."

"What about their families?"

"Assuming they even know where they are when released or left for dead, the families don't take them back. That's why groups help them to care for their abused bodies. They die of infection and injury less often."

The journalist asked, "Don't you think you're messing around with the natural order of life there? Their cultural beliefs of survival of the fittest?"

"Survival of the fittest has no bearing on this issue, Mr.,"

"Carlton."

"Mr. Carlton. When you take members of one gender attacking and destroying members of another gender, we have another form of genocide. They may not all die, but their spirit, their mental health, dies. Their connections and place in society die as well. However you look at it, brutalizing and terrorizing people for your own selfish wants and desires is against the world's human code of morality." The man seemed unconvinced.

"Is there a geographic area you believe is not addressed at all?"

"Many. Maybe you could cover one of those once a year. The benefit is tremendous. The girls still battle the emotional trauma of social exile that we cannot remediate in their home environments. We have to recreate a society for them. I love that I am a small part of the work, and I look forward to my time at the clinic. The one area I wish we could allocate funds towards would be transporting some of the youngest ones to a safer community."

"How young?"

"The youngest survivor I have worked with was nine."

The room erupted in outrage and murmured conversation. Kayla let them work through some of their thoughts before returning to the end of the day and the last clips. She focused her attention on her seminar group as the final clip ended.

"The victims' families don't take them back because of the shame and the diseases they can carry due to the violence. These girls are so emotionally devastated due to cultural ideology on uncleanliness they often commit suicide. That or find themselves in situations where their only way of survival is to continue doing what their captors did to them. Except this time, they sell their own bodies, not have it taken from them. It is indeed a tragedy. Any final questions?"

"How did you get into this line of work? Is it a hobby?"

"Not a hobby. I found I was great at public relations, and I realized the projects I worked on were humanitarian at heart. I accepted an invitation while in college to work with this population. After graduation, continuing with that work made it hard to keep a regular job. I needed more autonomy in the workplace. I took this job, and it afforded me much more free time to do the things I also love to do. Like this seminar sharing my experiences."

"What about your personal life? What does your husband think about all the time spent

gone?"

She smiled wryly. "Unfortunately, that part of my life is underdeveloped. I'm not married. That is one of the side effects of doing what I do; you don't have time to form strong bonds. At least I haven't figured it out yet."

Someone shouted, "Maybe you need to find some ex-military guy, hot and protective to go over with you like in the movies."

The room broke out in laughter. Kayla smiled distantly, but she instantly saw the image of River's face in her mind's eye. Hot and protective described him to a tee.

Another question brought her back to the discussion.

"How did you find the group you're with now?"

"Oh, right. Anyway, after the first year, I discovered the humanitarian program, Hope That Matters. They focus on women and young girls who are at risk of slavery or the human trafficking world. The work looks different in other parts of the globe."

"Isn't it dangerous?"

"Well, it does mean I am more exposed to the seedier part of the population in the most dangerous parts of the world, yes. But if we don't help, then who will? No one has stepped up so far. It's why I do this to bring awareness to the injustices of the world, man's inhumanity to man if you will."

The next day, they did exercises and group experiences to bring home the way the girls felt. The families, the thoughts and ideology behind that part of the world, and why it was important to make changes. The journalist did not return on day two. The seminar was too far from home, so River called her, and they talked for over an hour. Her brothers were in an attached room to hers in the hotel, and she felt safe with them there.

"So, no new threats. This was over the top. I'm safe." Kayla would never admit that on more than one occasion, she was glad that she could look over and see Taren.

"I heard you had a journalist there."

"Yes. Tomorrow, when I talk about the kidnapping, there will be more. It was prearranged."

"Dammit, Kayla, why didn't you tell me?"

"Why should I? They come to all my events or nearly all."

"I don't like it."

Kayla laughed. "And I don't like that I have babysitters."

"And I don't like that I'm not one of them." The phone was silent for a moment. "Kayla, come back with me to Port Refuge."

"Oh, you don't want me to do that. I'll be at Dad's."

"Just think about it, okay?"

"Okay." Her breath quickened, her heart began its typical pounding around River.

"Good. I bet I can change your mind."

"We'll see. Look, I need to go, get dinner, and go over my last day. It can be emotional, and I need my rest."

"And I have this dinner thing to go to before I send them all off to do their final department planning, which I will then need to approve. I might arrive after you. It depends on when I finish and the traffic. Why don't you go home with the guys, and I'll come to get you from there?"

"You don't have to come by. I'll stay there."

River was quiet. "I'll see you after I get back."

"But—"

"I said, I'll see you after I get back. Go to dinner. Good night, honey."

"Night."

As Kayla lay in bed later that evening, all she could see was River's face, hear his voice, feel his hands on her as he relaxed her to fall asleep. She slipped her fingers up to her breasts and teased her nipples like he did. Massaging, pinching, rubbing with one hand as his other, now hers in his stead, slowing slid down her belly to her thick patch of curly hair covering her pubic area. She tweaked her nipple and moved to the other, more sensitive nipple. She'd never noticed one nip was more responsive until River began to explore her body, and the zing was considerably more dramatic sometimes.

She traced the outer plumpness before delving between her folds to the slickness that appeared every time she thought of River, irritated or aroused, he always got a physical reaction from her. She circled her clit but didn't touch it yet. River had made her wait, and she would try to replicate that now because the orgasm was incredible.

She wiggled and licked her lips. The phone rang. She didn't hear it at first, but when the telltale ring that told her it was River got louder, she moaned and answered.

"It's late."

River was quiet. "It is, but I thought I would help you go to sleep. It seems like you have already started without me." Nothing from Kayla. "Nothing to say in your defense?"

"I didn't know you were going to call."

"No excuse, sweet cheeks. Am I right?"

"I was practicing restraint."

"Mmm hm. Let me describe what I'm going to do to you as punishment when I get you in my bed tomorrow night." Kayla moaned. "First, I'm going to take every scrap of clothing off your naughty body. Then, with nothing between us, I will kiss every erogenous zone you have, bit by bit, and a few you never knew you had." She groaned.

"Next, I'm going to nibble and lick those puckering nipples, squeeze and knead them until I have you writhing beneath me. Then I'm going to tease your quivering breasts with my mouth, fingers, and palms. Can you feel me, my impulsive lady?" A fast, shallow, breathy moan met his question. He chuckled with dark passion.

"When you're feeling desperate, I'll move on to kiss and lick your belly, nip your hips, hold you down at the waist. Then, having anchored you, I'm going to part your thatch of hair covering the promised land and inhale." He made an exaggerated sound in inhalation that curled her toes. "That earthy musk that I crave will herald your passion, begging I have a taste." Her whimper was sounding desperate. "Now, you earned this, remember. Can you feel me as I run my finger down your seam and delve inside?" His voice lowered. "You're slick. Naughty girl. You're being punished for starting to masturbate without me. I'll spank your pussy. I bet you can almost feel it. It stings but in a good way. I'll play with your reddening flesh and take some of the juices you offer me and lubricate your backside where I will breach your entrance, pumping my finger in and out, more lubricant, now two fingers. Feel the burn, the ache, the raising of your excitement. Now three fingers. Your juices roll back to your ass. You begin to meet me as I pound into you."

"River, please."

He continues without responding. "Next, I roll you onto your side as I paddle your bottom, one swat, feel the sparkling sting, now again, it's getting uncomfortable. Now again. You're achy, tingly, and want to come, but I'm not touching your clit, not yet. This is punishment, re- member? You want to come, don't you?"

"Oh, God, yes. Please let me."

That dastardly grumbling chuckle again. She was going to implode. "Slowly rub your clit, circle, and circle as I return to continue to take your ass with my fingers, put your finger in your sheath, put two. Spread them, Fuck yourself. Take your fingers from your clit and pinch your nipple. First one, then the other." He paused. "Now touch your clit again and put your fingers where they are most needed. That's it. Where are you putting them?"

"My nipples."

"Good, pinch and pull, spread your legs wide and keep them spread. Do not move them. Now tease your clit, fast, hard, bring your- self off."

There is a moment of heavy, short breaths before the fireworks be- gin. Vaguely Kayla heard a grunt on the other end of the line. Then a hiss as River released his pent-up breath. He found relief with her. As they begin to simultaneously slow their breathing, River cleared his throat, but his voice was raspy anyway.

"Good girl. Good night honey. Sweet dreams."

"Good night." Kayla rolled over and never moved again until morning.

DAY THREE OF THE SEMINAR was nearly half over. In a few moments, they would break for lunch and then reconvene to hear her tale of kidnapping. Kayla had thought long and hard about giving out details they had kept quiet for so long. She decided to tell most of it but still keep a few bits back. She and River had thought about what she should keep quiet. They chose to share the information about the items she had left behind in the taxi when kidnapped and that were subsequently returned without explanation. The team was told they had never found the taxi or its driver, but if that were true, returning things she left inside could not have happened.

River called her over lunch and gave her a pep talk. "We've gone over what you won't say. The rest is up to you. Tell it. Don't tell it. The story belongs to you because you experienced it. Don't let anyone make you feel as though they deserve to hear all the details. They don't. It's a gift you are bestowing on them and not an obligation you are fulfilling. Remember that and that you have help if you need it. I'll see you tonight."

The guys said they would be listening and watching. Robbie was recording her talk, and Taren was in his usual spot by the door. He watched every participant and journalist that came in and every place the contentious ones sat. He had his earpiece in and settled back for the next couple of hours. So far, so good. Nothing had happened during the whole workshop.

"... Before anything more horrendous happened, a team of military men came to rescue us. By the time they got there, it had been over a day, but I can tell you it felt like a month. The team of men followed, watched, and waited until it was safe. Just before we were going to be taken where they were selling us, Major Bennett and his team arrived to save the day."

"I have to tell you that while we were with men who had risked their lives for us and we were grateful, trekking back through the jungle when we had little stamina left was difficult." Kayla filled in more de-

tails and finally finished her story. "The other women were from different countries, so their embassies handled their return home. I was returning to the same country, so I rode home with the team. I assure you,
it is more excitement than I want to repeat."

Kayla could see her rescuer clearly. River's irises were a warm umber
rimmed in a deep chocolate brown that looked almost black. He was
intense and all business, and yet kind as they tromped through the
woods. On the flight, he was more than she expected.

She pointed to a young lady about college-age with her hand up.
"Do you remember any victim particularly, Ms. Rhea?"

"Yes, several, but most recently, on my last successful trip, I had a
part in saving a young girl. She'd been stolen from her family, and after
a year or so in captivity, I found her, used and discarded. The girl's nipples were pierced, her labia pierced, and her clit circumcised." Kayla
could not imagine the pain. "Not to mention the crude tattoo on her
arm, acquired in anything but sanitary conditions, identifying the cruel
taskmaster that owned her. The mutilations were all good ways of assur-
ing the girl would not run away until they tossed her aside."

The pushy journalist raised his hand. "Did you get all of your things
back after you were rescued?"

"All of my things? You mean like clothes and things?"

"Right, and equipment, phones, cameras, medical supplies, those
things."

"For the most part. The supplies were for the villages, so they had
already received them just before we arrived in-country."

"How do you know? I mean, anyone could have intercepted them."

"True, I would normally have seen them when I arrived, but this
time, I had to rely on the workers there who said they received them."

"And your personal items?"

"Are personal." She looked up and away from the odd man trying
to force another question on the floor.

Another hand went up, and she gratefully went to it. "Why do you call them mutilations? Plenty of people, including Africans, choose one or all of these things purposely."

"That is the difference. If you choose those things, they are adornments. But if they are forced upon you, the degradation and horror are overwhelming, and they become mutilations."

"After you found her, then what happened?"

"We got her medical help, a place to live with missionaries native to her area, and she started school. Her parents had named her Adia, which means a gift from God, but after this, she would be hated, not considered a gift any longer. With her permission, I changed her name to Aisha. It means 'a new life,' and that is what I hope for her. I believe she actually kept both names. It's all about choices."

"How is she now?"

"The last I heard, the now fourteen-year-old is flourishing. I intend to check on her myself soon." The question and answer time filled another thirty minutes. "Well, it looks like time is up. Thank you for your attention. I loved sharing with you all. For your final exercise, in the next week, take photos that speak to you and tell me why. You have the class-specific email. Thank you."

Kayla did love this part of her life, but she was anxious to get out in the field again. She needed to update her information. What Kayla had refused to factor in was with the raised notoriety, those she exposed were not happy with her. Robbie and Taren didn't have to tell her she had stepped on toes because the abusers told her themselves.

Now, River had joined the group saying she had to stay put until they identified the message sender. Some of the earlier messages were a little disturbing, but she chalked it up to just talk. Only the last one had disturbed her.

Cleaning up after the last person had left, Taren picked up a piece of cloth and began to tuck it into her backpack. Kayla became still.

"Taren, where did you get that scarf?"

"On the ground, why? I just assumed it was yours."

"It is, but it wasn't returned to me when I was kidnapped. I dropped it behind a rock at a crossroads so that I would hopefully be leaving a trail for our rescuers."

"Are you sure, Lala? Maybe River had it and slipped it in your bag. Or one of the ladies here had one like you. I mean, it can't have been the only one in the world."

"Maybe. Check to see if my initials are on the tag." As he unfolded the scarf, a bit of paper fell out. KSR was on the tag. The note said, "Some tenacious plants grow when put in hostile soil but not for long."

"Damn." He hit his Bluetooth device and began shouting. Robbie ran in, and Taren stopped demanding things on his phone long enough to point to Kayla. Get her and your gear out of here. Now, and go straight home. I'll finish up here."

Kayla raced over to Taren. "No, I want to see what's going on. Everyone is gone. It was a message, I get it, but I can stay and clear up. We can all leave in a few minutes. Please?"

Taren groused at the person on the phone. "She won't go. Sarge, I can't, oh, well tell River I can't do that to a grown woman, especially my sister. And later, I want to know why he thinks it's an acceptable solution. We'll be on our way within the hour. We still need to get to the hotel."

Taren shot his sister a curious look. "Grab your gear from the podium and around the room."

"What can't you do? And what about River?"

Taren ignored her question. "Leave the desk in the corner to me. Move it, girl."

"It's better if I do the desk because—"

"Dammit Kayla, just do as I say for once."

She turned to stare at her brother as he ran his hand through the thick strands of his hair. She saw his frustration with her, but what she focused on was his fear. His body was tense in a type of protective mode. She'd seen that look when River had discovered the email. Kayla nodded and turned to the podium.

"Thank you. Now let's finish this and get you home. I think I'm beginning to understand River better, now." She heard her brother's frustrated chuckle.

The trio gathered at the side door where the security guard would meet them to let them out. Kayla caught the look that Robbie had given Taren. There was more, and she instinctively knew she didn't want to see it. Kayla was fuming. How dare someone try to scare her into leaving those women to a fate worst than death. No one threatened her and got away with it. She would take her story in pictures to the biggest newspaper that would run her story and maybe do one of their own. It was time to make some noise.

Chapter Eleven

"What happened?" asked Sarge as his three children came dragging in the door after seven.

Taren looked at his father and said, "Let us get in the door."

"And I'm hungry," added Robbie. "We grabbed something right after we started back, but the traffic was hell. It took more than an additional hour." He dropped the gear in his hand and headed for the kitchen. "You can talk to me as I eat."

Taren took that opportunity to carry his equipment into his office. Kayla hugged her dad and asked if he'd heard from River.

"No, and that man of yours has some explaining to do. Letting you go, setting all this up without the go-ahead from me. That is not how this man's Army works."

"Dad, it's not the Army. And the boys agreed. So, that was that. I didn't agree, mind you, but I guess what I want doesn't really matter. I'm thirsty. And I need to call River."

"Doesn't anyone follow orders around here?"

No one answered. Grumbling to himself, Sarge followed his daughter to the kitchen.

As they entered the brightly lit room, she thought she needed to start preparing for another trip. And as much bravado as she could muster wasn't enough to settle the flutter in her belly. Hesitant fear descended over her like a shroud. *No one is going to stop me from getting the news out to the world.*

She stood in the kitchen and sent the email that she was ready to sell her story to the bigger news outlets who had asked to see it. Her exclusive received their email after they had sent the contract and would be publishing next week. Whoever got back to her first with enough of an offer had themselves a follow up story. She would show those bullies that she would do what was right. Even as she resolved to take up the mission again, she swore that it wasn't trepidation's cold fingers that raced up her spine.

The group ate a makeshift late-night snack in the living room when River arrived, weary and worried. He walked straight to Kayla.

"Hey, baby. You okay?" The looks her family gave River was almost comical. He knew they would back up any threat with brute force if necessary. Sometimes it needed finesse.

She smiled at him and shrugged. "I'm fine. They're just words."

Taren said, "Yes, well, they're threats, and the scarf was two threats."

River sat next to Kayla and pulled her in tight without any resistance. It did his male pride good to feel her relax and hear her sigh of relief. This one was not getting away from him. She was the first he'd wanted to keep, and she'd be the last. First, they had to deal with this threat. He looked over at the other members of Kayla's family, who stared at him hard, but said nothing. He counted that as a win.

Taren ignored the looks and asked, "What did the message on Rob's computer say?"

"If she returns, she will die."

Kayla wiggled. He was holding her too tight. "And what else were you talking about, Taren? A scarf?" Kayla sat up. Good choice because he was likely to crush her if it was bad.

Taren lifted the scarf from beside him. "Kayla had this in Somalia but left it on the ground as a clue to their direction. She didn't get it back. It was on the floor, and inside the scarf was a note." He handed it to River.

Before River read the note, he said, "We didn't find a scarf. We followed the trail and had a fairly good idea where they might be going;

however, missing a big sign like this is highly unlikely in both directions. We found a water container."

That started some grumbling. River looked at the note and read the
words: "Some tenacious plants grow when put in hostile soil but not
for long."

"Okay, what's the plan?" River asked.

All was quiet for a few ticks of the clock before the room exploded
in all kinds of conversations. Sarge was demanding answers that no
one seemed to be able to adequately supply. Taren was issuing his sister
edicts, and Robbie was pounding on the keys of his laptop, not even
raising his head as he interjected ideas. Then there was Kayla. She was
giving as good as she got while storming over to whoever had irritated
her. River began to corral his own thoughts, made chaotic by the family
squabble. He walked out of the room, and not a soul noticed. Good.

Grabbing the whiteboard and colored markers from the wall, he sat
at the kitchen table to begin writing, drawing lines, erasing. This is what
he did best, build a strategy of attack. He needed to look at this situation like any other mission. It was hard because he loved Kayla. Damn,
he did love her. And there was going to be nothing that stopped him
from keeping her safe: not the terrorists, not Kayla.

Eventually, things calmed down in the other room. River decided
he could bring them in on his planning. Walking into the living room,
he found four silent, brooding people in various stages of unraveled
moods. He quietly walked over to Kayla. He was going to get this main
part out of the way first so they could move forward.

"Kayla, come sit next to me, baby. I've been working on how we
should approach this problem. First, under no circumstances are you
going back to a place you are targeted for a kill." His harsh words drew
shocked responses. Sarge stood to speak, and River raised his hand.
"Not yet. I need to get this out first." He turned back to Kayla once he
had her seated on the sofa next to him. "I love you. I have for a long
time, and why it took me so long to figure it out is anyone's guess. I in-

tend to live a long, happy life with you, and you will help make that happen. Understood?"

She widened her eyes. "You mean it?"

"Every word."

"Okay."

"Okay?"

She nodded. "Okay."

River spent a few seconds reading her sincerity and saw it in her eyes. He placed gentle lips against hers before sitting back to tackle the next bit of business. He reached for the board and stood up.

"Right. Now we can start."

"Now just a minute. I have a few things to say," said Sarge. River sat down again and waited. "I'm not sure you have what it takes to make my daughter happy."

"Dad." River patted her knee.

"Let him speak, baby."

"I haven't known you well enough or long enough to know that you're the right man for my only daughter. It's going to take me a while to figure that out."

"I understand how it must feel, your only daughter leaving home to be with the man she professes to love and who loves her. But Kayla is well into adulthood, and as am I. We are not children with fairy ideas about beds of roses and sunshine paving every day."

"Hey, maybe I do."

River smiled and dropped a quick kiss on her lips. "Shush. We'll talk about that later." He turned back to face Sarge. "We will fight. Probably tonight. We will disagree on big and little things, and we will learn to compromise, but that's our work, not yours. I will be careful and protect your daughter, giving her more sunshine than rain, but we won't get along if you don't allow us our space."

"Kayla?" asked Sarge. "Honey, don't you think declaring yourself is a little soon?"

"When did you meet mom?"

"Soon after I arrived at my first duty station, and I get what you are doing, but it was different for us. We were older."

"Mom was twenty-one. You were twenty-four. So, it was a little more than 18 months from meeting to the "I Do's." River and I met when I was sixteen and again when I was twenty-one. If River hadn't been called away, we would have played house the night of the first Foundation Event I attended. Then he rescued me. Next, we met again at the Foundation Event a few months ago. And now we have progressed to where we are now. Dad, I am twenty-seven now, nearly twenty-eight. That means I have been acquainted or known River for over a decade. It's enough."

"I guess you're right. But I'm going to watch for the signs that things aren't good."

Kayla moved to hug her dad, and Sarge opened his arms to give her a landing spot. When she moved back to sit next to River, Sarge turned on his business persona.

"Now that we are through that, this is what I think. I'm not sure about who, exactly, but I've narrowed it down. The camera and things were given back to Kayla even though we were told the cab and driver were never found. Obviously, that was a big error in judgment. Who had access to the hostages' bags and items? The men from the foundation and the police."

"They had a local guide and interpreter, too," added Sarge.

"Okay, and him. Who would have had access to the scarf and know it was Kayla's?"

"The kidnappers," said Taren.

"No, because I dropped it when they weren't looking. If they'd have seen it, someone would have gone back, and they didn't. Believe me, I would have known."

The implications of how Kayla would have been made aware of the fact that one of the captors had found her scarf was evident on each man's face. Robbie continued.

"And then there was the recent photo that meant someone was there or at least close enough and at an angle that they could take that photo of the group before you boarded."

"We need to look at the first photo again because it can tell us more than just the location," said River. Robbie began pounding keys.

"Now, we need to divide and conquer. This is what I was thinking for this week."

The plan was soon set, and Kayla, being too tired to stay awake much longer, began to dose as they discussed passenger lists, agency lists, and more.

River looked over at her and put his hand up. "Okay, refer to the board if you have time to do more. Things won't happen overnight, but we *will* figure this out."

"Good," said Kayla with a loud yawn, "then I'll be able to go back."

"We'll talk about it after we figure this out. Go grab a change, and you can come back tomorrow to get more."

"But I was going to work at the apartment tomorrow."

River dropped a kiss on her temple. "Cute. I told you no more staying alone. The housekeeper comes in at eight and leaves at five. I'd take you to the island, but I need to stay in town for another week to follow up on the Gala. I'll spend a lot of time with you, but sometimes I'll be at the office. You'll have plenty of quiet time to get your projects done. Now hurry, it's late, and we're all tired."

She was too exhausted to argue. Hurrying, she grabbed the overnight case she hadn't unpacked and threw in panties, a clean bra, yoga pants and several tops. Enough for now. Kayla wanted to challenge his take-charge attitude, but in her state, she was happy to let River take over. They would iron out the independent details later.

In less than an hour, he had her tucked into bed with him spooning her protectively. "River?" She said as she yawned.

His sigh was indulgent. "What, baby?"

"You're on my side of the bed."

He chuckled. "Guess we will have to rearrange the bed because that side is closest to the door."

"So?"

"So, I can't see if someone enters the room if my back is to the door. And before you ask, I know you're safe, but I still have to do it. Habit."

"Oh. I guess I'll have to figure it out then."

"You do that."

"You don't care?"

"Nope, so long as the door is in my sight. Now go to sleep." He leaned into her and kissed her neck. "Better hurry or I'll think you want to fool around."

"It's after midnight."

"Mmhmm, best time."

She giggled as he gave her goosebumps from his nuzzling. "Goodnight."

"Goodnight."

The next few days went past in a whirlwind. Kayla made connections to see who wanted her follow-up article at the best price and distribution. She set up a few more speaking engagements and sent her info to the gal who did publicity for her. She loved the Condo view, and on Wednesday, as she was finishing her work for the day, a woman walked in as though she owned the place.

"Oh, hello, you're River's girlfriend, right? Kayla?"

"Um, yes. I guess you must be Chandra, his sister."

"Yes. What gave it away? The striking resemblance, the stylish clothing," she asked as she indicated her yoga pants and an overly large tee shirt. "Or, is it the beached whale impersonation?"

Kayla laughed, "The whale impersonation, definitely."

"I figured. Not the bold fashion statement I used to make, but Jake, or Jacob as he likes the rest of the world to call him, would skin me alive if I put on heels." She smiled and cupped her mouth with one hand, speaking in a stage whisper. "And frankly, I'd have to agree. Not a good idea."

"Yes, good choice." Kayla agreed with a smile. "Can I get you anything?"

"Yes, new feet, a non-aching back, and a flat, svelte belly again. Otherwise, water would be nice." Kayla nodded and went to the refrigerator for two bottles. "I hear you have taken up residence."

"Oh, um, kind of, but only at River's insistence. I know it's your shared place in town. Does it bother you? I could easily go home, or to the little apartment I have."

"Stop. I'm not entertaining here these days, and from the looks of it, other than you, neither is my brother. That is all we really use this place for. And sleep. If I have to be here for long days, I stay here, or if we are working through the weekend, I stay over, but since Jake and now little sprout take up most of my non-working hours, I'm not here much. Someone should use it. And besides, you're the first one he has brought here to stay the night."

"Oh. Well, that you know of, you mean."

"No, I mean ever."

"He is helping my father and brothers try to figure out who is harassing me."

"He's good at that kind of thing, but don't delude yourself into thinking that's why you're here. He's helped the search and rescue group in Port Refuge, and occasionally, he works with that group on Crystal Island, so I can tell you, he only does what he wants to do. Did you see those women paw him at the Gala? That, my dear, is normal."

"You were at the Gala?"

"Nope. It's just what happens when River attends these things."

"I don't need any more of that kind of attention, I can tell you."

"I imagine not. Don't worry, things will work out. But, if you hang out with my brother for much longer, I'll think you are going to stick around. River doesn't play. He is serious about his relationships. That's why he has only had you and one other one in the last ten years. The rest are one night stands. Literally."

"What happened?"

"I think she was more interested in forever, and he wasn't ready. And before you get it into your head that you have to be careful with him, don't. River is older, more experienced, and in a completely different place in his life now. And he is so much more opinionated. If he was done with your relationship, he would say so to your face." Chandra looked at her watch. "Oops, gotta go see mom before Jake gets back. Charlie, my watchdog, is waiting. I'm close to my due date, and neither Jake nor Charlie is happy about me doing too much." Chandra headed to the front door. "Nice meeting you. I'll see you soon."

"Okay. You too. Good luck."

The door closed on Kayla's final word. She wondered what it would be like to have another woman to chat with as a friend, maybe even a relative. Friends were not hard for Kayla to make; it was keeping them that was challenging. She had so many other things she was doing, maintaining them was difficult. Even close friends were more work than Kayla wanted to put into it. Now she felt the deficit because now it would have been good to talk about her life with someone. She would need to find a way to keep friendships alive enough to have a girl's chat with now and again.

Checking the time, she expected to hear from River soon. Kayla made some inquiries and found there was going to be another Hope That Matters trip. Sarge and the boys would flip if they knew, and she wouldn't tell River, either, but she was making plans. The group would call her back with the information she requested and send a copy to her email. It was close to six, and the housekeeper left at five but had made cannelloni. The fixings for a salad was waiting to be assembled. She wondered if River was going to be late.

Kayla decided to make one last check for her students' final assignments in her email before tossing the salad and throwing the dinner in the oven. The song heralding River's call had her singing before she answered. "Kayla, where are you?"

"Um, where you left me?"

The relief was loud in his voice. "Good. I'm running late but will be there in about half an hour. Put something on to ice, and warm-up dinner for us, will you? Do we need anything?"

"Nope. I'm good."

"Okay, I'll be there soon."

Salad made wine chilling, and entrée warming, Kayla tidied up in the master bathroom. As she passed her computer, she thought she would check to see if her information had come in.

"And there it is. That was awfully fast." She opened the file labeled, "Somalia." Just then, the front door opened, and Kayla went to meet River. She would read it later.

The dinner was good. They loaded the dishwasher together. "Do you want the leftovers for lunch tomorrow?" Kayla asked River. He hesitated. "Oh, sorry. The boss probably doesn't take leftovers from home for lunch."

"Yes, well, you'd be right, but only because I'm doing lunch meetings most days or business lunches. I don't have either of those things tomorrow, so that would be nice if you will put it in a microwaveable dish."

"You got it. Why don't you go and take a shower while I finish here? We can watch something for a little bit unless you have work."

"That sounds great. Hey, I don't want you to feel awkward about all of this. It's new for both of us, but we'll figure it out."

"I know. It does feel strange but good. Go take your shower."

"Right." He bent down and devoured her lips before he went back to the bedroom. Once Kayla was satisfied, she remembered her email and thought she'd do a little social media and then check her messages.

River was out sooner than she had expected. He looked gorgeous, all hard lines and a tan Kayla had no idea how he got at the end of winter. "That was fast."

He pulled her into his arms as she stood. "I didn't want to waste too much time."

"No?"

"No." Another warm kiss landed on her lips. River glanced over her shoulder. "What's this?"

"My email. You've been monitoring it, remember? I just thought I'd look one last time to see if any of the news spots wanted my follow up story before I distribute it wide."

"I wanted to talk to you about that. You're already in the crosshairs of someone. I don't want you to put out your story yet."

"Good thing I'm an adult, then."

"Kayla, hey, wait, what's this?" he leaned around her so he could click some keys on the computer. "Somalia."

"Oh, that is just one of the news outlets that I've been in contact with." Why did she not think he'd see it. He was monitoring her email.

"What the hell? Who sent you that email? Hope That Matters? That is the group you were over there with the last time." River was not happy. His displeasure came through loud and clear.

"Answer me, Kayla."

"I..."

"Did you look at it?"

"The information?"

"The damn email."

"No, I was going to, but," she shrugged. "You beat me to it. What's wrong. Look, I know you said I shouldn't put my stuff out yet, but—"

His voice was stern, and Kayla knew that tone. River was in protection mode, and she had learned to just ride him out, but it was so hard.

"River, honestly, it's just an inquiry, an email."

He pointed to one of the easy chairs he had in his bedroom, and she sat down. He was on his phone with lightning speed. "Rob, its River. Hang on while I try to connect with Zayden."

"Zayden here."

"Zayden, this is River."

"How the Hell—"

"No time for pleasantries. I have a situation."

"Shoot."

"Rob, look at Kayla's emails for this afternoon. You'll find one from Hope That Matters."

There was a whistle. "River, we have to find who this is. I'll run the normal tracers, but last time we came up with a lot of dead-ends."

"Right, I know. How about going from the organization? Maybe that would yield someplace to meet up with. Hell, that isn't my area of expertise, it's yours."

"Zayden, let me bring you up to speed." He took a moment to fill in the blanks and then went over the clues.

"Check the secured message I just sent you. Baby, tell us again what you did this afternoon."

"Okay, well, I sent out an information pack to see if any of my typical news outlets were interested in the story before I send out wide."

"Okay, then what."

"I called the mission agency and asked about future trips. The receptionist said she'd have someone send it to me, but she was new and didn't know how to find my past information. She said no one was available to help her, so she'd need my email address, and she would pass it on."

"Did they call you back?"

"No, just emailed me. River, I haven't even seen the email yet."

Without speaking, he picked up her laptop and brought it to her. She stared at the screen, trying to suppress the shiver of fear that enveloped her.

"River, that is our home for some of the girls. Is that real? Did someone really go in and do that to them?"

"I don't know, honey, but it's a good chance they did."

"Oh, River, that is my fault. Someone wants me to stop so badly, they will slaughter the girls I help. We can't let that happen."

She felt his arms surround her, taking some of the fear away. She needed his strength right now. The horrors of the world seemed to close in on her, and she was going to lose her dinner. Her strangled cry must have alerted him because River let her go. Kayla raced to the bathroom, where she proceeded to empty her stomach. The cold tiled floor felt good on her cheek as she laid her face against it. Suddenly, she was lifted and taken to the sink where the water ran, and a wet washcloth touched her face.

River made nonsensical sounds that soothed her while he dampened her hairline and behind her neck. Then he handed her a toothbrush with paste on it and stood behind her as she cleansed her mouth. When she was ready, he scooped her up in his arms to take her back to the bedroom. Sitting her in the chair again, he asked quietly, "You feel better?"

"Yes, no. Oh, I don't know if I'll ever be okay again."

"You will, but we have some work to do. You with me?"

She nodded. "Yes."

"Good." He kissed the top of her head and dialed again. The three-way call was soon resumed.

Zayden, who had always sounded so businesslike whenever she heard River and he talk, spoke gently to her. "You okay, Kayla? Do you want us to handle this ourselves?"

"No, I need to know what's going on."

"Okay. Good enough. River, so tell me the new things."

"These are the things we have right now." River went over the photos on the tarmac and the photoshopped picture of a dead Kayla. The mysterious return of the electronics. Then the scarf this weekend, the reporter knowing just a little too much, the computer message left at the workshop, and now this."

"Okay, so the common link is this Hope group," Zayden said.

"Right," said River.

Kayla spoke up. "And they changed our flights but didn't tell Sarge so we could coordinate."

"Did everyone's flight get changed?" asked Robbie.

"Well, we were all there at about the same time, so it stands to reason."

"No, it doesn't have to. See, you might have been the only one with that change. Everyone else might have already been on that plane," said Robbie. "I can verify that."

"Sure, but if they were targeting me, why not just have me come in alone?"

"Mistake?" asked Zayden.

"No, this was all very well orchestrated. I still haven't figured out how someone unauthorized emailed Kayla on her interoffice mail."

"It's possible. Hack in, and you're there, really." Robbie was clacking keys as he spoke.

"So now what," asked Kayla.

"Now we figure out who sent the email and then if that person truly sent it or was their account hacked as well. We also figure out how they got your calendar information and email addresses." River hugged her.

"Kayla's phone. It's likely bugged. They can get everything from her phone," said Robbie. "I'm on it."

"Zayden, I might need you to help put this together for me."

"My team isn't sanctioned outside the States, but I'm available," said Zayden, "off the books."

"Thanks. We have guys we can use from Sarge's group, but I'll need someone who reads me," said River.

"Right. Call when you need me, and I'll set it up."

Phone down, he turned and asked for Kayla's phone. "River, I need it."

"Not if they're tracking your every move with it. Let me check."

"It's been nearly a year and a half. It can't be something I don't already know about."

"And now you have your story to share, you have photos from earlier that you hadn't used before, you have names, places, events, all in that little exposé. You are talking to the media, which, except for the month after the kidnapping, you have kept quiet. You are a renewed threat to whomever you have upset in the first place."

"But why so long? I mean, some wacky emails in the first months but then nothing until that one with you at the studio."

"I imagine they thought that you were scared off and no longer a threat to their operation, and now they know different. The scums wouldn't know unless they could track you somehow. The only way they could do that effectively is from your phone. That you lost, then was miraculously found and returned before you left the country."

Kayla stopped pacing and returned to land heavily in the chair she had vacated earlier. "Damn you, it makes sense." She pointed to the dresser behind River.

He walked over to Kayla, crouched down to kiss her, bringing her head to rest on his chest. "It's what I do for a living even in the civilian world. I puzzle things out, I plan, then I help people implement. I enjoy it, but not when it involves those I love. I love you, Kayla. If I can't figure this out and come up with a good strategy for stopping this terroristic attack on you, then I need to find another line of work."

"But it isn't your fault or your problem."

"No, not my fault, but it's my problem now. Let's get this phone in the safe and then have it checked out tomorrow. We will find a way to end this."

Chapter Twelve

Robbie's serious voice resounded across River's phone receiver. "Yes, I'd say, if she had this phone on her since the kidnapping, then she didn't make a call, receive an email, or go to the store without the people on the other side of this tracking device knowing about it."

"That's what I was afraid of but hoped I was wrong. Can you take the device off?" asked River.

"Honestly? I could, but I would feel better if we got her another phone," said Robbie. "What I can do is see if I can trace any of it. Sometimes they can put on a thing like a tracker but don't know all the in's and out's of keeping the tracked from becoming the tracker."

"Great. Hopefully, that's the case here, but I have a feeling it isn't. These people changed flights, organized the snatch, and then, almost too easily, we were able to get the group back. It was all too neat. Can we keep it? I think we might find we could use it when we're on the hunt for the person or persons responsible for everything."

"Yep. I'll just turn it off. Want me to get a phone sent over to Kayla?"

"Nope. I'll get one. Zayden is flying to Seattle when I need him. He's going to help us put an end to this cat and mouse game we find ourselves in. Kayla needs closure. Can you talk to Sarge and get a meeting together? I have a plan I want to run past everyone."

"You got it. Hey, River, take care of my baby sister."

"That's what I'm doing. Get that meeting going, okay?"

River knew things were going to get hot quick. He had to put his head solely in the game. If he didn't, he'd lose control, and it would become more than any of them could deal with.

A phone was delivered to Kayla at River's apartment with a note from him.

"Here is your new phone. The other was being tracked. I'll tell you all about it when I get home, or you could give Rob a call. I'm in meetings all day, but you call my cell if you need anything. I can push stuff to my assistant or the vice-chair if you need me. I'll be home at about six."

Love you, R

Home. To her. The last months had been something she had only dreamed of until now. Kayla loved that River made it part of every day to make sure she was taken care of, but ever since that night after the threats and finding that scarf, he'd been obsessive. He worked on her dilemma with a single-mindedness, making her safety the primary goal, which didn't always bode well for her. She wasn't entirely happy about some of the side effects of a man being so intent on your life, the main one being her lack of privacy.

River was never hesitant to declare he loved her, generous with both his time and his energies. After finding the phone had a tracker in it, he was burning the candle at both ends, which worried her. He was looking tired, had become sharper on details and in his responses to her. It was becoming almost scary. Although he said he lived for missions like this, she knew he was working too hard. They fought and made up most nights.

She'd known long before she ever lived with him that she was falling for him. Kayla looked back and realized she'd reached the point of no return. Hell, she'd been half in love with River from the moment he'd rescued her, and likely longer than that. She would have to figure out the over-protective bit. For now, it was a side effect she could handle.

River had put all kinds of events and meetings off for her, and she felt guilty when he did. This time he couldn't. He was slated to go to Africa to oversee the wells the Foundation was putting in with their engineering designs. At first, he'd decided to send someone else like he always had, then he seemed suddenly eager to go. Something was up. Tonight, he came home with all kinds of paperwork, and he obviously had a plan he was going over in his mind before leaving. It was now or never.

"I can go with you, River."

"Kayla, for the last time, no, you can't. We have gone over this, discussed it, and fought over it. The answer is still no. Rob told you he saw communications, just this week, that explicitly named you as a target. You would be in danger over there, and you aren't going again until things calm down, if ever. I think I've put things together, but I need some final intel to know for sure."

"I'm a grown woman, River, and if I want to go, then I'll go. Besides, what if they never calm down? What if you never find out who is targeting me? Am I supposed to live my life this way forever?"

"You're are also my woman, and if I say no because your safety is in question, then the answer is no. It is going to be 'no' until I say it isn't."

"That's keeping me here when I could help. And I would be able to see the girls that I've been helping. They must think I've abandoned them."

"I said we're going over there to do Foundation work and to try to eliminate the threat. I can't do that with you around to worry about. I'll send someone over to that area to check on the girls and take some photos so you can see for yourself. We're substituting most of my Foundation people for Sarge's people, and Zayden is tagging along."

"I haven't had a threat since that last email just before you found out about the phone. I've let Rob screen my accounts like a child so you would get that I'm not in danger. It was a flavor of the month thing, and that was it. It's over."

"Wrong, you're going to be their biggest coup if they get to you. Stop pretending this is nothing. It isn't. You need to understand that the only reason these people have backed off is because they aren't tracking you. They might not have figured it out yet or because you've kept a low profile since then. I don't know, but what I do know is that you sold your work, and in the next month, it's going to be big in the investigative reporting world. And you will be front and center again. They cannot afford that."

"I'll stay low. I won't cause one bit of trouble. I'll do what you say."

River stood and walked over to Kayla. "Baby, I can't risk your life. I would never recover if you were hurt."

"But I'll be careful."

"Like last time."

"Yes, like last time. I didn't do anything out of protocol. We have gone over this, and you know it wasn't my fault. It was a set up from the moment I signed on."

"Are you looking to get killed? You. Are. Not. Going." His hand cut off any words she might be forming. "Find another place in the world, but not there."

"When are you leaving for Africa?" Kayla hoped if she changed the subject and got his dates down, then she could go around him. She would only stay for ten days. He said he would be gone for two weeks. It would be tight, but it could work.

"The first week of July, and I know what you tried to do just now. Let me be very clear, baby. If you go back to where you were or even close to that area without me, I will have you removed, kicking and screaming if necessary. Then, when I have you safe, I'm going to light up your world by making your ass a glowing beacon of red, ground your ass to the island, and hire a bodyguard. Don't push me."

"Then I'll find another place to work."

"Good; focus on that."

"The men in my life are too overprotective. Sarge said he would hide my passport. Robbie said he would put me on the no-fly list."

"Because they love you. Good ideas, by the way. We are all going to be very protective until this whole thing is over."

"What do you mean, over? What are you going to do, exactly?"

"Catch us a terrorist."

RIVER GOT THE CALL the day after he landed in-country. He was preparing to leave Mogadishu for the two villages receiving their wells before taking a side trip with Zayden and Sarge's people to go on a hunting expedition. He knew some areas to start.

The call came from Kayla. "Hey, what's up? I only got in yesterday. Miss me already?"

Sarge was furious. "Kayla is gone."

"What? Gone? Gone where?"

"Where do you think?"

"Fuck. How do you know?"

"They called the numbers she left for an emergency to verify they were good numbers. You probably got a call too. Hope That Matters is in Somalia, Congo, and other places in the region this month. When I came here to check, she'd left you a note. Some very pregnant woman let me in."

"My sister. Go on."

"Kayla didn't explain. Evidently, this is a conversation you had previously, but she did say where she was going. She also left this phone saying you probably had it tracked too."

"Where is she exactly? Nevermind, I know." came the grim question.

Sarge continued. "I'll send the coordinates to you and an interactive map to your phone, just in case. Taren and Gunn are already on their way. They're bringing additional gear for you guys because it is probably going to be Fourth of July worthy when she lands."

"And when is that?"

"This afternoon. The thing is, the group said special trip arrangements were made for her, but when I pressed them, they said they would have to get back to me. Something is damn fishy."

"They're ass-deep in this whole mess. Kayla was right; I put a tracker on her new phone. A helluva lot of good it will do now. That woman is too smart for her own good. I can go to where you expect her to be if I don't get her at the airport. Send me all the intel you have. We will have to regroup."

"Got it."

After a few more words, they signed off. River loved her. He'd fallen too deep to dig his way out. Not that River wanted to, but he would be damned if he let her place herself in this type of danger again. He would never recover if something happened to Kayla. Maybe it was time to make a baby, to give her someone to nurture in a safe environment. River shook his head. He was going mad.

He'd lock up her passport. Should have done it already. Have Robbie put her on international watch lists for Africa. He'd take her everywhere he went from now on, so this never happened again. After River painted her ass cherry red and made love to her until she didn't possess the strength to fight against his protection. He'd tie her down at night and to him in the day. Yes, it was the best strategy, and he should have listened to his instincts earlier. Too late for that now.

The wait was the most difficult thing River had ever done. He met with the project manager on the wells for the Foundation. River had expected to go with them on this first meeting, but his timetable had been tossed. They were working from plan "B" now.

River checked the designs with the engineer and sent him on his way. "I'll catch up as soon as I take care of this business. Sorry, but you've done it without me before. I'll be there a day or two behind you."

He hoped.

River had slept with Kayla two nights ago, and she'd agreed she wouldn't go to this region. He'd be the boots on the ground for this gig without a doubt. River was glad to have Zayden with him, and with Rob and Sarge at the com center, her other brother and cousin on their way, and a good handful of well-trained operatives, he'd make this work. He had no choice. Kayla's life was on the line.

What he couldn't understand was why she came anyway. She was frightened. They'd talked about her genuine fear. He checked his phone like Sarge had mentioned, and there was no call. It might have been a mistake when they called Sarge. She didn't shy away from confrontations, so he wondered why.

Yeah, this was personal. He was tired of watching, time to man-up and take some action by putting a ring on her finger. That was after he made sure she was safe and out of the country. He also intended to impress upon his adventuresome freedom-fighting, female rights activist woman that his word was her new law.

Robbie called and said that Kayla wasn't on the flight that they said she was on. When they confronted the agency, they swore she was. When Robbie had given them the actuality of it all, they appeared genuinely stymied. River's brain imploded. *Time to settle down and go hunting.*

"I think someone is using the agency as a cover," said Robbie. "They didn't even have a trip this month to Africa. It was put on their calendar yesterday. *After* she had a ticket. I'm trying to see where she is and who paid for her ticket since we can't seem to get that information from them."

"Where does that leave us?" River's mind was clicking into place, but he knew the value of patience.

"I'm checking the most likely flights, and then I'll go wider, but she'll probably be in-country before I find her. She could even be there now."

"Damn. Okay, I'll grab the guys off their plane and take off. We'll contact as we can."

Finally, Taren and Gunn landed. While waiting, River formed his plan and discussed the best way to get in and out. Assignments made, equipment gathered, rendezvous agreed on, they jumped into the jeeps he had previously acquired and took off. They arrived at the coordinates of the village just at dusk.

When River inquired about where he could find her, a wizened old villager informed him they called her *marwada waalan*, the crazy lady but with affection.

The man went on to say. "It is a strange thing. Why would anyone let *marwada waalan*

come with only a few men? Her family must not be good protectors. Maybe they are weak men."

How very wrong he was. If the villagers only knew how hard her family had tried to keep her under wraps, it would've been another story. Had the tribesmen known Kayla refused her father's help, and, this time, she snuck away against the advice and admonition of all who loved her, they would probably not allow her back. He would make sure he let them know he was her man and forbade her return. Archaic but effective.

"These are Kayla's rebellious years." Her father told River when explaining why he allowed her to do what she wanted but under his watchful eye.

River called bullshit. Kayla was spoiled, and because of a reckless sense of purpose, she was putting her life in danger. Yes, she had waited for a year and a half before returning, but she had also sold her series of photographic articles, opening up the book of revenge again. Kayla thought it was an acceptable risk; River did not.

Just before he'd gotten on the plane to come, some of the men in her photos were identified. They were wanted men, all right. She had effectively told where these notorious men were and what they were doing. This whole mess ended here and now. He prayed his girl didn't die for her cause.

River, Zayden, and Robbie had discovered, through all their connections, that an American was in the mix, and it was not Kayla. Also, the agency had gotten a rather large donation right after Kayla was taken. Who was their link? River turned back to the man in front of him.

The old villager seemed to have more to say. River wanted to know what that was. "Where did you say she went?"

His question was met with a sad face and a shake of the man's head. River's gut clenched. With a tight chest, he waited for the answer.

"She interfered with the soldiers this time, and they hit her." The man swung his arm in demonstration. "They said if she wasn't gone by tomorrow, they would take her with them."

"So, she left," River said as a statement of relieved certainty.

"Oh, no." The man shook his head vehemently. "She is still here and is not going to leave." He finished the story matter of factly. "When they are done with her, she will die."

That hard reality sent cold fingers of fear up River's spine. If the scenario happened, he had no doubt the old man was completely accurate. River's voice hardened.

"Where is she?"

"Come, I'll show you. Maybe you take *marwada waalan* with you?" the man said hopefully. River simply nodded.

River's make-shift team was scanning the area for some of the men the old man described, possibly hiding in the other dwellings. Zayden went with him.

Sitting on the ground, he saw her, and his heart did a leap of joy and crashed in fear. Her hair was pulled back into a high and tight ponytail, not unlike his sister used to do as a kid. She looked so innocent. Her cheeks were deeply flushed, and dirt smudged her shirt and shorts.

He could feel a smile break across his face. It wasn't often that he experienced the wonder of humanity, and Kayla's compassion and inner strength in the face of danger captivated him. He was attracted to her for so many reasons. This is why she defied him. Not for her own profit, but because she loved these girls and feared for their lives more than her own. He could learn from her.

River had witnessed the best and the worst during his military career. His woman would always be about the best in life. He watched with great fascination as his slip of a girl, in the middle of chaos, calmly spooned watered rice gruel into the eager mouth of a small child. River couldn't imagine eating it himself but knew it was nutritious, and the child was so malnourished, he probably couldn't hold anything stronger on his stomach. And frail. He was too fragile.

A young girl, about fifteen, came out to take over the feeding. Kayla reached out and hugged her. The reaction was one of hesitancy, as though the kind human touch was foreign and almost frightening, certainly unexpected. Kayla smiled at the baby and extended him to the young girl who tried to smile back out of a face that was clearly unpracticed in it. He loved Kayla so much. Angry words spoken in Arabic brought River back to his situation and hers. He made himself known.

"River," came her stunned greeting. "I'm sorry," she indicated the small group, "but I'm not going back yet."

"Baby, I understand, I do, but you don't have a choice."

Her response became more militant, and he responded in kind. "I'm here, and now that I am, I refuse to be forced to do something that I don't agree with."

"Listen, I think I understand, but you don't have that luxury right now." They discussed the incident earlier. "Good, I know you understand why you have to leave today."

"I heard all this earlier from the villagers and Gunn a few minutes ago. I should have known you would be with him. I can handle myself. I do every year. If you understand, then you won't ask me to leave."

"We have reliable evidence this trip wasn't made by the agency, and we are sure of who wants you dead. Someone is pulling the puppet strings, using the agency as a front. This mess was an inside, outside, and topside event. You've done a good job of pissing people off, sweetheart. Taren is here too, watching out with a few other guys so I can get you out of the village."

"Who is the silent one behind you?"

"This is Commander Wellesley. Zayden."

She nodded. "I figured. None of you are going to make me change my mind. Someone has to stand up for these girls, River." Tears welled in her eyes. River wanted to give her what she asked, but he couldn't.

"Kayla, we'll launch a campaign to get the word out. I can use the Foundation to make people listen, but only if you come now under your own steam." He continued after she shook her head. "Listen, baby, as I said, these are not normal times. These guys will kill you without blinking an eye. In fact, they are likely paid to do just that." He looked down at her hands, "at least your hands seem to understand the full issue here. They're shaking. Your whole body should be shaking. Look, what good are you going to be for these girls if you're dead? There is no martyrdom in this part of the world."

River's voice went low and even, but it was obvious to any who could hear him that there would be trouble if his words weren't heeded. Kayla didn't appear as though she would take good advice. He didn't want a confrontation but didn't mind if it got his woman out of harm's way. Unfortunately, it was her stubborn pride that wouldn't let her step away from the situation on her own. He didn't need her permission.

Kayla began to stand after his last warning. He noticed the girl had taken the baby back inside. Kayla turned to walk away but stopped suddenly and flipped around, putting both fisted hands on her hips. River had an instant desire to laugh, except this was extremely serious, and the sound choked in his throat. There she was, standing hands on hips, her face contorted in anger, defiant to the end, and she was no match for the majority of the men surrounding her. She reached out quickly and cinched her ponytail tighter, eyes flashing. God, he loved her spunk.

"Look, I don't need to leave. These people never bothered me before, and except for the last time, it isn't going to happen again. I admit I was scared to come back. Terrified to leave the plane and get in a car and come here. But I did it because someone must show the girls they care. I doubt those thugs are going to bother me now. It's not like the last time I was here. It feels different. I hadn't gotten to the village yet when the kidnapping happened before. Here in the village, it's a show of bravado by wannabes, nothing more. I bet they don't come back tomorrow."

"Are you willing to take the risk?"

She looked into River's pleading eyes and knew she was jeopardizing a future with him, and she almost changed her mind.

"Yes."

"Well, I'm not, and I don't really think you are either. These wannabes, as you call them, are not the only ones with obstinate bravado."

Was he right? Was she really willing to risk her life and his? No, not his, or the others and maybe not hers. She was so confused between her desires in this situation and her hope to do more for the girls. She had to leave River now, or she would lose her courage. Kayla jerked around to walk away when she felt a vise-like grip on her upper arm, stopping her in her tracks. It took her a moment to process what was happening. She reached up with her right hand to peel his fingers off her bicep only to be met with an even firmer hold on her other arm. He turned her. It was what she would have expected a death grip to feel like.

"River, that hurts. Please let me stay. If I go, it'll be as though they won."

Kayla jerked her arm hard, trying to loosen it from his grasp when she got no response. He loosened his hold enough for Kayla to yank her arm out. She immediately reached her hands over to the opposite arms to rub the painful impressions left by his grasp. River pushed her hands away as he rubbed the spots in comfort. She didn't look down or break his gaze. She shivered as his voice got that familiar low dark quality about it.

"Kayla, don't make me force you."

"Honey, I don't know if I can, in good consciousness, leave now."

She watched his eyes squint. He was thinking. She'd seen 'the look' enough times when River didn't get things the way he wanted. He was scheming. His look of determination had returned. It was going to be a fight. Part of her, most of her, wanted to go with him. The other part still wanted to walk away from River, effectively blowing off his offer for assistance and his analysis of the situation.

Not leaving with him now would end their relationship; she had no doubt of that. Maybe even her life. Kayla couldn't help but admit she was scared. And deep down, she feared he was right. Even if he wasn't, could she survive without him in her life? Not just for today, or this week, but for the months and years to come? She loved him, he was a good man, and she had given up so much for so long for others, couldn't she choose herself for once? Choose what they had and could have, now?

She knew if he hadn't challenged her, she might have considered leaving with them quietly, but the dye was cast, her prideful path marked. She didn't know how to back down now, though she wanted to, acknowledged that she should. She gave him a pleading look to understand and take control, a control she rarely gave up willingly. River would say she needed to work on that. He would make her practice releasing her pride, give up control, and do the right thing. Could she do that?

Chapter Thirteen

He stepped in and kissed her hard. The kiss tasted of desperation and fear.

"Listen, little girl, I don't know who you think you are right now, but you're not going to put an end to these men from coming back. As much as I admire what you're trying to do, you're not going to be able to stop them from taking whomever they want, including you. And they *will* be back. Think about it for a moment. How did they know you were here?"

"I don't know. They shouldn't have."

"Right, baby. They were sent here." He blew out a frustrated breath. His forehead touched hers. "One or more at the group, Hope That Matters is in on this. We have narrowed it down as to who knew things about you before getting on that plane. I'll explain later, but I promise you, you won't be here when the hired assassins return. We have many things to work out in this shit fest, but I don't have anything to work out about how much I love you. I want you to be happy, but nothing will happen in this country between you and me, except what I say will happen. *Fahmo?*"

She smiled her relief. No choice, she had no choice. Kayla wanted to agree with him so badly. "Yes. I understand."

"Good answer. Grab your gear." She saw his face relax for the first time since she'd defied him.

Before River stalked off in the other direction, presumably to initiate his plans, he left Kayla with a parting remark. "You're not going to be here tomorrow when the soldiers come back. Say your goodbyes, sweetheart. When you're safely away from here, we'll finish this."

"Promise you will let me visit the girls."

"I promise I'll try." River stopped and strode back to Kayla. He pulled her close for another quick kiss, and this time there was a relief. River turned to instruct those of his group to be ready to leave at first light.

"Major, shouldn't we go now?" River hadn't heard that title in a while, and he appreciated the respect. He looked at Gunner.

"Kayla and I are going tonight, but I need it to look like we just left out before the goons come back. If they follow, it will be you they track, giving us a little more time. There's no doubt we're being watched."

If there was trouble, they were to go to the backup plan "C." He wanted it to look like Kayla had finally come to her senses, the militia had scared her out, and it had nothing to do with the American military or ex-military in the area. Gunn and his brother Axel, whom River had never met, agreed. Taren was pissing mad at his sister, but River intervened.

"Get your head out of your ass, Taren. We don't have the luxury of you having a sibling squabble out here in the middle of fucking nowhere."

"Yeah, I get it, but when we are out of this hellhole—"

"When we are out of here, you are not going to be more than a brother who worries about his sister because she is mine to take care of, not yours."

"The hell—"

"Let it go, man. I'm going to marry Kayla and make adorable babies with her. She's already mine." Taren hesitated and then nodded and walked off like the good soldier he was.

The little village settled down when darkness fell. True to her routine, Kayla left soon after dinner to the segregated hut considered unclean. She shared it with some of the young girls who'd been defiled by the troops and traffickers. This village allowed them to live in this small place and scratch out a living. Kayla worked hard during the day, and normally it didn't take much for her to fall asleep, but tonight she was keyed up waiting for River to come for her.

She was afraid and appreciated how stupid it was to trade her life when nothing good would come of it. She realized River was right when he said she was no good dead. River loved her, and he would keep his promises. She could make such a big difference overseeing the distribution of information on a larger scale. She no longer felt safe and didn't want to anger her lover.

She knew there were men in the village who stayed awake during the night to listen for danger. She always felt that it was security until today. Now she knew any one of them could have been paid to kill her. Tonight, nothing made her feel safe except River. Always River. He wasn't taking her freedom; he was keeping her safe. *Time to wake up, Kayla, and time to quit being so selfish by drawing the soldiers to the village, endangering more children.*

Kayla got up and dressed. She needed to find River before he came to her and frightened the girls. She'd be sorry to leave the village, but it was time. She grabbed her small survival kit and smiled as she left the rest of her things to the girls. They would be excited about the assorted luxury items and foods she'd brought. She wished she could watch their excitement. Another day.

Stepping out of the little hut, she ran into something hard. Abject horror overtook her as she went into automatic fight mode. She'd trained in self-defense, but it was true what the instructors drilled into her. The only useful defensive tools are the ones you use without thinking because when you are fearful, they are all that will come to your mind.

She dipped out of the arms that surrounded her, quickly returning with a kick towards a vital organ. Her attacker was ready and blocked her. Every defensive kick she executed, he countered with ease. Then a hand covered her mouth, and an arm wrapped her tight to his body. Before she realized it, she found herself being carried out of the village with her mouth gagged.

Kayla knew that if a villager saw them, they would not stop a man carrying a woman. They'd tried too many times before and been thwarted. They'd let it happen. She also knew it was her own fault. She'd put herself in this predicament, but she refused to go without a fight.

Sweat and body odor permeated the air around them and slickened their skin where it touched. She twisted violently to try to gain her release from her captor's arms. The man placed three hard swats to her shorts covered bottom in quick succession, and she instinctively stilled her movements but yelled her objections.

"Hush, woman, it's me." River followed his actions with menacing words softly spoken. "Quiet now, unless you need a long-term gag to help you."

She shook her head. He reached back and untied the bandana and pocketed the cloth.

"Damn, woman, you have a nasty kick."

"You scared me to death.

When she attempted to demonstrate her displeasure again, River placed his hand on her bottom.

"Kayla."

She relaxed. She fully expected River to make good on his threat if pushed. He turned his head and kissed her cheek.

A familiar chuckle was heard behind them. Kayla hissed at Taren. "You let him do that to your sister? Scare me like that? Just take me?"

"This man has my undying respect. He can handle the beast. And yes, you deserved it for what you put us all through. You deserve that and more."

"What happened to familial connections? Protection? Little sister?" she hissed.

"He is your man, sweetheart. There isn't another person in the world who could love you like this man does. Only a fool would stand in the way of his protection. And I'm no fool."

A big warm hand belonging to River splayed across her bottom once again, and Kayla quieted. She could almost hear the satisfaction from both men that they could bring the situation under control with simply a well-placed hand. River had magic fingers when they were in bed. Why would it surprise her that there were even more dominant features in this man? It didn't, and she loved it.

THEY MADE IT TO THEIR vehicles and were relieved that the heavy-duty Hummers hadn't been tampered with. Then they waited for the rest of the team, led by Zayden, to arrive back in Mogadishu and their room before anyone discussed what they had found.

"Sorry we're a little late," said Zayden as the group dropped their gear. "Had a few visitors trying to crash our farewell party."

Gunner grinned. "The Commander gave us some tips on how to handle gate crashers. Effective. I'm going to love going through one of his training courses."

Zayden nodded. "Glad to help, but don't think that because we have a history, I'm going to go easy on your asses when they're under my command."

"No sir, I didn't think that at all." The guys laughed.

Zayden grinned. "Good." He turned to River. "Okay, brother, what's next? I've got a wife who gets antsy if I'm gone too long, and if I get back a little early, I get a reward." He wiggled his eyebrows.

"Can we just stop the good 'ol boy routine and tell me what's going on? Who's doing this?" Kayla demanded.

"Don't be nasty, Baby. It looks like Rob has brought his "A" game. I'm conferencing him in on my computer." Everyone sat around the room as River opened the connection. "Hey, Rob. Tell us what you have."

"I've got Sarge here with me, so we only have to hear it once. This last piece just came in. It's what we kind of expected, but now I have the names." Robbie cleared his throat. "Kayla, when you took photos of the men who stole women, did you realize that you had taken a photo of the leader?"

"Yes. At first, I thought he was one of the kidnappers, Ahmed, but after I got a closer look, it wasn't him."

"There was a good reason for the confusion. Ahmed, whose full name is Ahmed Aden Farah, is Osman Aden Farah's brother. Osman is the one you took a photo of as he was carrying off a young girl. Their father, Aden Farah Jama, one of the richest and most influential men in the region, has not been happy that you shared his son's photo all over the world. It also appears that he is in on the South American trade in the last few years."

"Okay," said Kayla, "So he was upset his baby boy got unwanted attention, and he was trying to live in the shadows, fine. He must have been the one who kidnapped me, right? Except Cumar was the leader. Ahmed was just disgusting and aggressive."

"Makes sense. Ahmed is the young, more immature son. The one with fewer aptitudes. But Aden Farah Jama wanted you kept out of the country so you couldn't share any more of your photos. It seems he knew that if he had you killed, they would look to him as the reason. He didn't want that attention. So, he contacted one of the members of your team, Mr. Hermon Perez Sanchez."

"What? No. I've been going on these trips with him every time. It couldn't have been Hermon, Robbie."

"It was. I traced the emails and the tracker to a little town in Paraguay. Remember that picture that was sent to you of one of the girls at a brothel? Well, that was in Paraguay. Mr. Sanchez has been the go-between for Mr. Jama and the prostitution rings in Paraguay for quite a few years. The society was a good cover for him."

Tears streamed down her face. Kayla turned to River and buried her face in his shirt. She felt the heat from his body folding around her. "How could he? He was the one who called the police."

"All part of the cover. Sanchez and Jama didn't want to kill you but scare you into never coming back to Africa. The police were paid off so they wouldn't look for you, as they often are in places where the money is short, and crime is high."

"So, let me get this straight," said River. "Sanchez had been using the trips to get girls that Jama helped to kidnap and transport to South America. Sanchez was paid his fee and kept his hands relatively clean, as did Jama. So how did you find them?"

"Like I said, I traced the tracker and one email, the last one, back to Sanchez. Then, I went to the family pictures of those we could name in the photos. Using facial identification that a friend of mine helped create, I began to look into the other pictures Kayla took. The pieces started coming together, and the connections came quicker. The last piece was a phone number on Kayla's old phone. It went to the estate of Jama while she was with the kidnappers."

"Someone used my phone to call Jama? Didn't they think I might see it?" Kayla asked.

"I have always told you, most criminals are more stupid than they think," said Rob.

"So, after you found Jama and the connection with the photos, the first names of the kidnappers, and connected it with the family names, things fell into place," repeated Zayden.

"Right. The only one with the phone was the man who gave it back to her. If you look at the photos closely, in one of them that someone took, Sanchez was returning the bag with her tracked phone."

"But what about the scarf?" asked Kayla. She seemed to have recovered and now was as angry as she was sad.

"Ah, that was the easiest part. The reporter I contacted said he got an anonymous tip that you would be available for private interviews. They said you would be happy to get the scarf back, but in your opening, you made it clear that until your work was out, you would not speak to any reporters privately. Afterward, you would welcome the opportunity. He hung out thinking that was the public statement, not the private reality. Evidently, he was so angry that he had wasted the whole weekend, he tossed the scarf on the floor and left."

"It was a miracle my team hadn't left the city yet because it would have been two days before anyone else would be able to put boots on the ground."

"Oh, right, I forgot one thing that baffled me. It was an email to the police chief, obviously bribed as well, about Senator Gregovich's wife being kidnapped to bring in the American rescue team. Evidently, that was so Kayla wasn't killed, just frightened."

"That was why it was so easy to find Mrs. Gregovich. She was just a lure to make sure we were available to go find Kayla and her group. It was also why they almost gave the women to us when we arrived. Now, as for Kayla's group, why were they involved?" asked River.

"Accident. Their tickets were set for a few hours later but changed on accident to meet the change that was put in for Kayla. The receptionist was new and thought it was an oversight. The kidnappers didn't know who they were supposed to kidnap, so they grabbed them all." The room was silent. "Anyway, I sicced Interpol on them, and the appropriate officials have been alerted to suspicious activities."

"I won't ever be able to come back, will I?"

"No, baby, I don't think you will. We can't eliminate the problem without creating even more. This is a bottomless cesspool of filth."

"Can I at least see the women one more time?"

"I'll see if I can get a satellite connection set up for them."

"Thank you. I think I want to shower and go to bed now. Thanks, Rob. See you in a few days."

FINALLY HOME, KAYLA worried. River said very little to her after they found what the whole mess was about. He held her, but he didn't make love to her. To be honest, she probably wasn't ready to give into him, anyway. She certainly wasn't prepared to initiate anything. She was the saddest she had been in a long time, and it was difficult to deal with it. Had she lost him anyway?

When she refused to allow him to cut his trip short because of her, he'd gone silent. He'd placed her on the plane with Zayden, Gunner, Axel, Taren, and the rest of her father's crew. She watched stone-faced as she taxied away, mirroring his look. She stopped watching when he was no longer visible to her. She slept most of the flight home and cried the rest.

After she returned to the condo, things were off. Kayla discovered just how angry at other humans she could be. She couldn't shake the feeling that she, in some way, aided men taking and destroying young girls' lives just by being there with Sanchez. Irrationally, she hated herself, was angry with Robbie for bursting her bubble, and even at River for being there when she needed him.

Storming around the condo for a day didn't make her feel better. Kayla tried her studio, but she had found in the past months that she worked best at the condo. That realization made her even angrier. She should put in her notice at the apartments. She returned to his penthouse to feel closer to him. She missed him no matter how out of sorts she felt. Her favorite wine didn't help, nor did chocolate. Her sappy chick flicks made it worse.

Finally, she settled her tears and started to work on her pictures in the study where River had lovingly created a shared workspace. There was another room available, but he said he wanted her near him. She was in the place where she needed to be, doing what she loved. The rest would have to work itself out. Soon the words flowed and wouldn't stop. She told of the pain and horror of being used for the destruction of others. She shared the story in intimate, catastrophic detail. That's where River found her on day four, sleeping with her head on her project table.

"Hey," murmured River in her ear, "I'm home."

Kayla jerked awake and wiped her mouth with the back of her hand. In her half-sleeping state, she didn't have the filters of logic to stop her words.

"What are you doing here?" River stepped back as though she had bitten him. She shook her head, adamantly. "I didn't mean it."

"Which part?" he asked warily.

He was hurt and uncertain. Kayla had never seen this side of River, and she hated it. Explain, she had to find her way through a foggy brain that had too much worry and too little sleep.

"I haven't slept," she said.

"What? At all?"

She shrugged. "Me, either."

"Really?" she asked in a cheerful voice. "Oh, that didn't come out right either. I'm sorry you haven't slept." This was too stilted. River hadn't come closer.

"Well, I guess I'll find something to eat." He turned and started out the door.

"River." He stopped but didn't turn around. "River, I love you."

Now he turned. Was he going to tell her he didn't love her anymore or that she was too much for him? She had caused him an incredible amount of pain and worry these last weeks. He had left the military for a posh civilian world with a predictable life. She was anything but predictable.

"I love you too, but—"

"I know. I'm sorry. I'll change, I promise."

Tears streaked her face as he lifted her from her chair and carried her into the bedroom.

"Hey, hey, what's all this about? Don't cry, baby. I came home early because I missed you and wanted to make sure you were all right. I wasn't any good there with you here."

"I thought you wouldn't come back or that you'd ask me to leave because I was too much trouble. I gave your foundation, your family, *you*, a bad name. Please stay with me. I was wrong, I—" His lips covered hers.

"I'm sorry about my own behavior. I was such an ass when you flew out. I had a hard time letting go of my fear for you. I only wanted to get you home. I couldn't concentrate without you even though I knew you were being cared for. I gave up and came home." River grinned. "Actually, my engineer sent me home. I love you, Kayla Rhea."

"I was stupid to try to sneak behind your back and not make it easy for you to take care of me. And I didn't see all the mess that was going on around me for years. How could I have been part of that whole horrible situation?"

"Sweetheart, you couldn't have known. Don't you see? Your honesty and integrity was their cover. You expected everyone else was there for the same altruistic motives. They couldn't allow any hint of their operation to get to your ears, or it would blow everything. You would have no qualms about outing them."

"So, you don't hate me for complicating your life?"

"I welcome the challenge."

"And you won't be upset if I find another project?"

"I expect it. But there will be guidelines."

"Can we negotiate?"

"Probably every day of our lives. Anything else?"

Her tears were mixing with her smiles. "I'm having trouble with the bed. Can you fix it?"

"The bed?"

Kayla nodded. "It's lonely."

"I think I know how to fix that problem." His lips crushed hers.

"It's a start."

Chapter Fourteen

Six Months Later

How did she find herself over his hard thighs again? Right, it was Thursday. Sexy day. River had been working hard, they both had, and because of that, they promised each other that on Thursday nights because Friday's often had them wining and dining some investor or other, they played. For a woman who had never experienced spankings as a child, it fit into her life on sexy day so easily.

"River, honey, please? I've made safe choices for a while now so you can stop with the spankings. I obviously got your message. Your strategy has worked wonderfully."

Her whine did nothing but elicit a raised eyebrow from her man which, she just caught when going over his lap. It certainly did not slow his stripping of her clothing off her lower half or her honey slipping down her legs.

"I can see the results. I'm not sure we will ever end this ritual. It has kept my sassy wife sweet and obedient."

"Mm, but I get my reward afterward, right? It's been days since you've kissed me all over." Kayla wiggled her bum. "And I've been good. You said it was only until I kept safe." She continued to lie over his lap, wiggling her bottom as she spoke, her movements pressing her pussy against his legs and heightening her arousal.

"You are saucy tonight, woman. How about another type of spanking, the type you like?"

"Dessert first? Yummy! Does that mean maintenance is officially over?"

He sighed as though he was giving up a favorite toy. "For now. It's perfect timing actually because I need to check on the wells. I want to see they are working as they should and negotiate another couple of sites."

Kayla tried to roll off his lap, but his strong arm stayed her. "River, I could go with you. It would be great, really. I could check on the girls of the village, and take more pictures, get more information for my articles and be fresh for the next Foundation board meeting."

A firm slap landed on her upturned bottom. "Ow! That isn't the good kind of spanking!"

"And so, maintenance begins again." He landed three more swats. "No, you are not going with me." A flurry of purposeful swats landed on her plump derriere.

"But, honey, it would be perfect. Ouch! You could protect me and... Ouch!"

The End

USA TODAY BEST-SELLING author, Alyssa Bailey, is a dyed in the wool Texan dividing her time between cowboys and wide-open spaces and absorbing the beauty of Southeast Alaska.

Alyssa loves writing about happily ever after romances between intelligent, sassy women who are not afraid to make a stand and men confident enough to give his woman space but Alpha enough to keep her safe. All couched in a little mystery, humor, and suspense.

She writes historical and contemporary love stories devised to leave you with that *book hangover* we all crave.

Find Alyssa Here

Sign up for her Newsletter HERE[1]:

Facebook Group Fun[2]

Twitter:[3] @blushingalyssa

Blog/web page:[4]

Bookbub[5]

Instagram[6] @alyssabaileyromance

Amazon[7]

---

1. https://landing.mailerlite.com/webforms/landing/z6h6m3

2. https://www.facebook.com/groups/635273300210359

3. https://twitter.com/blushingalyssa

4. http://alyssabailey.com/

5. https://www.bookbub.com/authors/alyssa-bailey

6. https://www.instagram.com/alyssabaileyromance/

<u>Goodreads</u>[8]

7.   https://www.amazon.com/Alyssa-Bailey/e/B0113ST54E

8.   https://www.goodreads.com/Alyssa_Bailey

More from Alyssa Bailey:

Lairds, Lords, and Little Ladies: Georgian Historical, spicy

Lord Thayer's Choice

Lord Ashton's Decision

The Black Laird Requires

Lord Kendrick's Obligation

CHASE ABBEY SERIES: Regency, Sweet and Spicy, suspense

 Lord Barrington's Minx

 Becoming Lady Barrington

 Lady Caroline's Defiance

 His Improper Lady

SAFE AND SECURE SERIES: Contemporary, suspense, spicy

 Saving Sharlee

 Saving Jessie

THE O'CONNOR SERIES: Contemporary, Rancher, Saga, Spicy

 Liam & Jocelyn's Story-

 Her Sweet Complication

 Liam's Lessons

 Loving Liam

 Ciarán and Katherine's Story

 His Gentle Persuasion

 Rancher's Creed

 Katie Consents

 Quinlan and Cheyenne's Story

 Quinlan's Quest

Accepting His Way
Her Balancing Act
Kelli and Parker's Story
Meeting Her Needs
Kissing Kelli
Keeping Kelli
Cián and Molly's Story
In Pursuit of Molly
Freeing Molly
Forever Molly

CLEARWATER RANCH -Contemporary, Spicy
Piper's Plan
Camille's Second Chance
Josie's Refuge

LONE WIND SERIES: Contemporary, spicy Native American
Reclaiming Clover

TAMING TEXANNA -American Historical, Marshall, Native American, Spicy
Cowboy Welcome- Contemporary, Spicy

ANTHOLOGIES (VARIES)
Sweet Town Love
Historical Heroes
Hero to Obey

Cowboy for a Cause

GUARDIANS OF REFUGE (Contemporary Military Spicy)
SEAL of Refuge
The Strategy of Love

__MULTI-AUTHOR BOX SETS__ (Heat Level Various)
Love, Christmas 2 Movies You Love
Love, Christmas 2 Recipes
FREE Book Bites 11
Christmas Shorts
Irresistible Heroes
Tempting Protectors
Sexy and Seductive
Sweet and Sassy Summertime Vol. 2
Dear Santa: A Christmas Wish (Oct 2020)

WRITING AS TASHA WINTERS
__Captured Series__ **Fantasy/Sci-Fi**
Captured Obedience
Captured Desires
__Alphas in the Wild Series- Shifter Fantasy__
Wild Alpha Fantasy: A Steamy Shifter Romance
Wild Alpha Promise: A Steamy Shifter Romance

Did you love *The Strategy of Love*? Then you should read *SEAL of Refuge* by Alyssa Bailey!

Too Good To Be True

Alesha Campbell loves her Alaskan island home but two years after a painful break up, she fears she might be terminally single. Then she meets the new guy in town. The widowed Naval officer extricates her from a sticky situation and stole her heart, but he seems too good to be true. That's because he is.

When the Navy offers SEAL Commander Zayden Wellesley the career opportunity of a lifetime, he accepts. On a recon trip to his new station, he meets the woman he never knew he needed and sets about wooing her. Things are going well over the short trip except for one little snag: He neglected to inform her he had roommates.

Zed did plan to tell Alli before she found out on her own, however, his roommates took matters into their own hands before he could talk to her. Can Zayden save his career and his budding relationship without upsetting the delicate balance he was already maintaining?

Read more at alyssabailey.com.